Wanting to Belong

Mike Jenkins

seren

seren is the book imprint of
Poetry Wales Press Ltd
Wyndham Street, Bridgend, Wales

© Mike Jenkins, 1997
reprinted 2000

A British Library Cataloguing in Publication Record is
available from the CIP Office

ISBN 1-85411-210-4

Cover photograph: Al Jones

The publisher works with the financial assistance of the
Arts Council of Wales

Printed in Plantin by CPD (Wales) Ltd, Ebbw Vale

Wanting to Belong

This book is dedicated to Pete, Jill, Clare and Gareth.

Contents

Acknowledgements

Some of these stories have previously appeared in *Planet, New Welsh Review, Swagmag, Cambrensis* and Radio 4.

Thanks to Bethan for choosing the title. Also to Mark and Faye – "Mule On!"

Wanting to Belong

Hiya! I'm Gary Crissle and this is my story, well some of it. I know my name sounds like rissole and rhymes with gristle, but if you're smirking you wouldn't if you saw me, cos I'm pretty solid, as they say round Cwmtaff. I've got boxer's muscles and I'm tall as a basketball star.

Gary is short for Gareth. I like Gary because it's more cool. Gareth sounds a bit naff, though it makes me more Welsh. It wasn't like a passport when I first came to Cwmtaff though. It didn't matter to them.

I got Gareth from my mam, who comes from here originally. She's small and blonde and nothing like you'd picture a typical Welsh woman to be. She met my dad at a disco in Cambridge. It must've been dark cos he isn't exactly John Travolta. More like John Revolter, I'd say!

The Crissle comes from my dad of course, and isn't the only thing he's lumbered me with. There's my teeth, which stick out like a cartoon rabbit, though my brace has trained them down recently. The first month at Pencwm Comp, I had it on. Imagine being from England and having an iron mouth as well. The stick I got was beyond. I never told anybody the name of the village I'm from, as it would give them more ammunition. It's called Horseheath. They'd have me born in a cowpat! So Cambridge was enough for me. When people talk about racism, I know it isn't all black and white.

(I'm writing now when I can. There's a terrible routine to my life, but it helps to get things down.)

It seems that Mark Rees was behind most of it. Sparky they called him. He was a small, scrawny boy into everything he shouldn't have been. Most kids in my class worshiped him, while most teachers couldn't stand him.

Sparky loathed me from the start. He was always nicking my bag and hiding it, so in the end I stopped bringing one to school. He got the others to go 'Oo arr! Oo arr!' whenever I read in class and even called me 'A posh twat' which is a joke cos my accent is real country, though I've picked up some Cwmtaff recently.

The crunch came when Sparky and his gang decided to jump me on my way home. He didn't like the way I was friendly with the teachers. He thought I was a crawler, a grass, but I never meant anything. I just wanted to belong.

Well, my mam was working all hours and my dad's job at Hoover's was on the line. Things were very strained in my house and I snapped at school that day. Although I'm strapping I'm not a troublemaker, but Mark Rees pushed me too far.

We had this supply teacher with a fancy voice, who was also from England. I felt sorry for him but couldn't sit there like a stuffed parrot while our set played up. He tried to make contact when he heard me, and I replied to be polite.

'Who do you support?'

'Cambridge United. They're great!'

'Oo 're they? Oo 're they? Oo 're they?' Sparky started up a chant that all his mates copied and the poor wimpy supply screamed 'SHUT UP!' as sweat leapt from his face.

I lost my head. I clutched the paper in front of Sparky (with only the drawing of a magie on it), crumpled it up and rammed it into his gob.

'Out!' yelled the supply, 'both of you. Out!'

I suppose he thought he was being fair, but what happened after was that a Deputy, Mr Lloyd, found us in the corridor mouthing and shoving each other, and he blamed Mark Rees cos he'd got a reputation worse than Ian Wright.

I didn't expect him to get revenge so soon. Him and his mates ambushed me in one of the alleys in Penôl estate, where we both lived. I didn't stand a chance against six of them, though I tried my best.

'Bog off back to bleedin England!' Rees swore as he kicked me to the ground.

I made out I was hurt more than I was by yelling hell and this woman stuck her head over her fence to give off to Sparky's mob. They gobbed at her and left me blacker than a copper's uniform and bleeding like a beaten boxer. The woman was nice and offered me a cuppa. I told her no and stumbled home.

There were plenty in school who didn't go along with Sparky, who knew he'd end up going down or killing himself in some stolen car. But in my form he ruled like one of the Mafia. His word was law.

I began to really resent my mother for being Welsh and for dragging us back here. My younger brother in Year 7 seemed to be having it easy though, cos he was sickeningly good at everything. He was called Ryan and was a left-winger and they nicknamed him 'Giggsy'.

I wanted to impress upon Sparky and the boys that I wasn't a swot. As my schoolwork went downhill faster than a freewheeling pushbike, my mam got a warning letter home. She threatened to ground me for at least a month that evening.

'I ain't staying in!'

'Get to yewer room, Gary!'

'I ate this crappy town and I wanna get back so I can see United every ome game. It's your fault!'

'Yewr dad'll ammer yew when ee gets ome. Now do as yew're tol!'

'Naff off woman!'

I slammed out and ran for my freedom. I ran towards town through streets which were carbon-copies. I ran past the bus-shelter where Siân Jones and her friends stood smoking. I liked Siân, but the girls she bothered with bugged me no end.

'Ey Gary, wha's up? Runnin from Sparky agen?' They cackled like demented chickens. Siân looked on, sad.

I didn't have a clue where I was going. All I ever did in the evening was have a kick around with Ryan and his friends. I thought of getting on a bus or train, but I was skint.

(Listen, I've got to go now and leave this for a while. Unfortunately, there are things to be done. Lights to be put out. Promise I'll be back.)

Anyway, what did I do? I carried on striding down High Street, till I heard this familiar voice calling out – 'Gary!

'Gazza!'

Gazza? Was it really referring to me?

And there, sitting on a bench was Sparky, ready for the taking if I'd been in the mood. He was a tiny ant without his gang: could easily be stamped on. I crossed over to him, more out of curiosity than anything. His eyes were glassy and he giggled for no reason. I could see how other kids were attracted to his cheeky eyes.

'Alright? Where's the rest then?'

'Revisin f' the exams, o' course.' I could see he was talking bull cos of his grin. 'Ow come yew're down yer. Not yewer scene.'

'I've ad enough. I'm runnin away!' Strangely, I found myself speaking like him.

'This is-a cheapest way t' excape, Gary.'

He took out a carrier-bag from under the bench and offered it. It contained a flagon. Sparky was a real alkie.

'What is it, meths?'

'Scrumpy Jack. On'y the ard stuff. Knock it back!'

He was standing now and practically pouring it down my throat. Before I knew it we were exchanging swigs and strutting through town. 'Lookin f' action,' Sparky said, though it was deserted as a wet winter Sunday.

'Don' worry Gaz, there's always one f—in plank-ead!'

I didn't know what he was on about, but the Scrumpy was doing its business and I was travelling far enough without spending a thing. I liked the way Sparky had changed towards me, though I couldn't fathom why. Maybe it was the booze. If so, I didn't want to be around when he got a hangover.

As we passed the taxi-rank and the station, he was babbling away like he did in lessons.

'Gary, yew carn elp bein English. Listen. I really liked the way yew stuffed tha paper down my gob. Yew got style. We could be a team.'

He began to sound like some gangster film. Nothing seemed real till we reached the rough and ready car-park near the railway line. Then he spotted something and flung the bag into a tangle of weeds.

'Looks as if someone's missed theyr train from Cardiff.'

His baseball cap was a buzzard's beak, as he clawed in his jeans pocket. What he'd noticed in the distance was one particular car, not a new job, but an Escort GT all the same. I could make that out and I was no expert.

When he took out a screwdriver I was dead scared. In fact, I was nearly pooping my boxers! The cider hadn't made me bold enough, but I couldn't let on or Sparky would spread it round school faster than teletext. Instead, I made out I was a professional.

'Ow about goin fer a better one?' I suggested, hoping he'd be diverted.

'No way, Gazza. This one's got no bells. Yew int scared, 're yew?' He stared, grin gone, eyes full of purpose.

'No way! Let's go for it then!'

'Yew wan-oo?' He held out the screwdriver.

'No thanks. You're the best, Sparky. Everybody says.'

I thought of legging it rapidly, but before I could say 'Yer come the cops!' he was into the Escort and he even had a key.

'C'mon, Oo Ar ol son. Le's mule!'

He called me Oo Ar pleasantly now. I felt accepted. As soon as I sat in the passenger-seat he put his foot down and screamed away like the cops were chasing us already. I belted up, but didn't feel exactly safe. Joy-riding's definitely not the word for it. I'd call it 'mental muling', except I'm not sure what that means.

He drove like a boy possessed, taking the roundabout by the Labour Club almost on two wheels. We flew under the railway bridge and out of town. The cider wore off in seconds. I knew he was more than half gone and though he handled the car like a bucking bronco, I could still see us getting thrown.

'Jus drop me off at ome fer a change of pants!' I gasped.

Luckily, the road was deserted as town had been. Everything was fast forward and my hands fumbled the dashboard for a hold button.

'Where we goin, Sparky?' I asked, trying to sound super-cool.

'Oo knows? An oo f—in cares!'

Then he lifted both hands and I closed my eyes and –

(Interruptions! There are always people poking their noses in here. I'll start my story again when I can. But with all the commotion going on I don't know when.)

I opened them and we were on the slip-road overtaking a lorry. Sparky was yelping and laughing his head off at me.

'I cun smell summin, Gaz, an it int the engine burnin!'

'Now what? The cops are bound to find out an I'll be for it. My dad'll murder me!'

'Right! Jes round Asda's roundabout, through Macdonald's fer a burger an 'en ram-raid-a gypo camp.'

'No way, Sparky, there'll be a huge great security barrier.'

'I ate em!'

'What? Security barriers?'

'Na, gypos! Worse 'an the English. No offence like.'

He sped round Blaenmorlais top and back downhill again. I saw a white car along the Heads of the Valleys which could've been the police.

'Spark! Look! I'm sure I seen the cops!'

'I'll go up the Bogey Road. We'll lose em tha way.'

He took a sharp left and I had to admire his skill. It was a Grand Prix to him.

'Better 'an shaggin, eh? Even with Siân!'

Suddenly, it was all ugly. I noticed the glint in his eyes when he mentioned her. I wondered what the hell I was doing in a stolen car with a boy whose gang had only recently jumped me. I didn't belong here either. He drove frantically towards the unofficial gypsy camp with its wooden fence. My dad had driven past once and my mam told me about it.

He swerved into the entrance and I instantly made a grab for the wheel. He jammed on the brakes, skidded and we hit the fence and a man standing just behind it. He fell with the impact as the car stopped.

Sparky reversed and accelerated up the hill, yelling a series of curses at me. Now he was truly mad and veered off the road onto the moors, our headlights picking out fleeing sheep and small ponies trying to gallop away.

'Orsemeat f' supper, Gary! Yew aven ad Siân 'en, I take it? Yew mus be the on'y one!'

The Escort rose, then dipped wildly into a pit. My body jerked like a fit. I couldn't see! Sparky shouted so loudly and painfully it razored my nerves. The car was motionless. I could feel damp spreading. I daren't open my eyes this time. I wanted to wake up somewhere else: at home, in comfort, by the telly. I wanted to rewind the tape and delete what had happened since I met Sparky.

Everything was frighteningly quiet. I kept on seeing that man we'd knocked over like a wooden pole, maybe lying dead.

If only I hadn't touched the wheel. Then I imagined Sparky and Siân Jones at it in the back of a car like this, and dared open my eyes again.

My jeans were blood-soaked. It was on my hands. I wasn't cut. Where was the blood...? Sparky embraced the steering-wheel. His head was deeply cut. I whispered 'Sparky' and shook him. No reply. His face was deathly white. I panicked. Releasing the belt, I staggered out. I stumbled back along the direction I thought we'd come, tripping over clumps of reed. Surely the road wasn't far? Luckily, it was a clear night. I swore and swore at Mark Rees, for every step a different word. I nearly crossed the road without realising it. A pile of tipped rubbish told me it was there. I followed it downwards and heard ahead another voice of panic, echoing mine.

I'd have to pass that camp and they could kill me, but it was my only chance of getting help. Maybe Sparky could be saved. I didn't know if I wanted him to be, but I'd have to try.

What could I tell them? What convincing story? I groped in the dark for one.

In the end, I didn't have a chance to explain. As I trudged towards the ramshackle camp among what looked like old waste-heaps, all I could hear was – 'Look yer's one! Quick, grab im!'

Before I knew it a horde of youths and children were coming for me. I went on, shouting 'Elp, elp! I need an ambulance, quick!'

There must've been blood on my face as well, cos they held back from attacking me. The young men grabbed my arms, the children my jeans, as if making a citizen's arrest and marched me towards a battered old van, parked over our skid-marks. Among cries for revenge like 'Give im a boot in the goolies!' I noticed how one man, who was holding open the back doors of the van, managed to pacify them.

'Sure he's hurt. Leave him be!'

His voice was authority. I was chucked like a sack of

coal into the back alongside the old man we'd knocked over, who lay groaning between two rolls of carpet. My head hit a sharp jutting edge of metal and began to bleed. I welcomed the pain. I deserved it. Absurdly, I began to wish I'd been injured more seriously.

'It wasn't me! I wasn't drivin!' I explained pathetically to the man who drove the van, who'd saved me from the mob.

(I can hear someone coming. I'm going to tell those kids to 'Bog off or I'll kick your eads in!')

It's later now and I'll tell you what happened. Bri, my Care Assistant came in. He saw me writing.

'Good news, Gar.... Oh, sorry! Wha's this then? Yew doin omework? I don' believe it!'

I rolled up this paper hurriedly, holding it tight, in case he decided to investigate. I've got a lot of time for him, but he does want to know everything.

'It's nothin, Bri. Jus letters, tha's all.'

'Okay! Anyway,' he says, eying me suspiciously, 'yewr parents want yew back an I think there's a really good chance of it appenin ... everyone knows yew've done yewr time in yer. T' be onest, it woz an ard deal in the first place.'

Brian put his hand on my shoulder and I had to swallow hard to keep down the tears. I squinted into the mirror and observed myself, thin and puny, for the first time genuine. Perhaps I should change my story? I wanted to hug him and tell him I'd never do anything like it again, but I couldn't be so soft even in my room with no-one watching.

'Thanks, Bri,' I said, thinking of Sparky half-dead in

hospital and with a chair-bound future ahead of him, and of others like him who'd go from probation, to fines, to prison. I thought of that old gypsy in his grimey, cast-off suit rattling agony in the van, each moan my guilt. I thought of his family who forgave me while I sat with them all night, willing the monitor to keep on bleeping his life.

I'll end it now, though I'm sure there are bits I've left out. Do I belong more in Cwmtaff? Well, I know where I don't belong that's for sure.

Trolley Down the Taff

I don't know where he came from. From Pluto perhaps. Or beyond? I do know he lived in the Homes, but so did Gary Crissle (and we all knew about him cos of Cambridge and Steve Butler on the back of his shirt). I do know he was stonkin' and he wasn't aware of it. His black hair kept springing up in curls no matter how many times he kept plastering it down. Me and the girls took bets on when it would stand up straight (the hair I mean!)

He wore the same Adidas trenchcoat every day. Teachers would need crowbars to remove it from his body. He was wiry, not skinny like Gary, and you could tell his muscles were tuned. He was hopeless at every sport, the boys in our class, 9B, would always say, except climbing up the wallbars and swinging on ropes.

Maybe he was one of those 'wild kids' I'd seen in films, like one with Jodie Foster in. Brought up in forests or something, discovered like a modern Tarzan and taken into Care. I wouldn't mind being his Jane, even if he only had three hairs sprouting from his chest!

It was his stories that really impressed me first. He never did any homework, but when it came to the usual rounds of 'Why not, Siân?' ... 'What now, Gary?' ... 'Go on, tell me, Christian!' ... then Chrissy would not go any shade of red as he told the most outrageous lies.

'Well, miss, sorry miss, but I ad to go an visit my dad in Ponty. When I got there ee took me out in is new car. It were a Ferrari or summin. Ee let me ave a go at drivin it an I knocked inta a tree.'

'So?' says Mrs Joyce, our Geog teacher, never giving up.

'Well, my dad grounded me miss.'

'So?'

'Ee wouldn give me no pen. Jest kept me in a room. Bread 'n' water diet. Like a prison, miss.'

'If this were English composition, Christian, you'd get a grade 'A' for imagination. However, this is Geography and unless you give me the exact grid reference of the damaged tree, you're in detention!'

'Oh, miss. It's true! 'onest!'

It didn't make any difference cos Chrissy never turned up to detention anyway. He had another story ready.

Which makes it very strange that he took everything we told him so straight. Perhaps he believed his own fantasies, so what we said was just as real. Perhaps he'd never grown up. When a new phrase came into our way of talking like 'Shirley Egg' – which was really a greeting – he picked up on it like a little kid wanting to play with someone else's toys.

One day he stopped me outside school as I was walking home.

'Siân! Oo is she?'

'Oo is oo, Chrissy?'

'Y' know, 'is Shirley Egg ev'ryone's on about. She mus be summin special.'

Like the others, I couldn't resist the fun. I touched him on the sleeve, whispering in what I hoped was a sexy way.

'Chrissy ... if yew wan', I'll arrange f' yew t' meet er. She's never in school, she's always bunkin see. I know where she d' go daytime.'

'Wha? Siân! Amazin!' He took out his fags, lit one in celebration and gave one to me. 'Funny name, mind, Shirley Egg.'

'Tha's jest er nickname, Chrissy. She got it coz she wuz-a first person t' egg someone on theyr birthday.'

'Onest? She mus be a real one-off!'

I soon had it sorted. Chrissy was to meet this Shirley Egg up the Miler, an ancient mile-long railway tunnel which was a haven for glue-sniffers, pushers and even devil-worshippers. Me and my friend Kar reckoned we saw the ghost of a boy who'd been knocked down by a train in there, but it could've been somebody messing. Kar claimed she went back the next evening and spoke to him and he was talking like Shakespeare, but she was into the supernatural and would say that.

Anyway, I persuaded Wayne Griffiths (who Chrissy hardly knew and was ace at drama) to dress up as a girl. On the agreed day we had dental appointments and such like. Me and Kar hid out the way in a big hole in the wall where the bricks had crumbled, while Wayne put on Kar's mini-skirt.

It was dead funny cos he kept slipping over and getting ladders up his sister's tights. He put on a real poofy voice. I think he liked dressing up though.

'Oooer! These yer rats keep gettin up me drawers, loves!'

We nearly wet ourselves giggling.

We were quite close to the entrance, but enough in the dark to fool Chrissy.

After waiting for ages our excitement was turning to mind-numbing boredom. Even Wayne 'Shirley Egg' and his come-on legs – as he tried to hitch lifts from passing ghost-trains – couldn't improve things.

All of a sudden, Wayne saw a figure on the path approaching the tunnel opening.

'Yer ee comes!' he said and hushed us. We crouched

back in our cubby-hole, biting sleeves to stop ourselves from bursting. Wayne leaned against the dripping wall like some prossie on the pull.

I could just see one boy appear at the entrance, then another shortly after. They didn't hesitate as Chrissy would have, but carried on down the Miler, stopping dead before bumping into Wayne.

I didn't recognize their voices. Me and Kar stared at each other boggle-eyed.

'Hiya love. 'ow much d' yew charge 'en?'

'We're skint, but we could pay yew in tabs, carn we Rob? Wanna drop some?'

'She's ewsed t' droppin summin else, I bet.'

'Ey, look at 'is, Rob ... boy's clothes. She must ave someone idden....'

I could hear a scuffle and the two boys shouting after Wayne, who must've given them a rugby hand-off to get away and protect his life (or his sex anyway).

Me and Kar were petrified in case they spotted us. We breathed in like we were ready to dive deep. If those two stayed, it could be for ages. Either that or they could go mental popping pills.

'Le's see if we cun catch er?' said one and they set off after poor old Wayne, who'd have to dash through Pwll village looking like a Welsh Mountain version of Madonna!

We waited a while, but Chrissy never turned up.

You know what? Next day in school he told us all about his meeting the legendary Shirley Egg. She'd greeted him by flinging an egg at his head and then they'd disappeared into the Miler for some serious snogging. Me and Kar even dragged him along at break to see Wayne, telling him he was Shirley and had nearly lost everything to prove it – those boys never caught him mind. But Chrissy thought we were bulling. That was typical! He wouldn't believe the truth! He described Shirley in detail, though not too many layers down! Funny thing was, it did resemble Wayne in drag.

The next thing Chrissy took up on was the bucket. We began to get tired of his stories and began to bother with Kerry Richards and his gang, who were into draw and stuff like that. Kerry was always on about having a bucket and Chrissy must've overheard him. He kept on pestering us all the time, so I told him that if you got the stuff for cleaning graffiti off desks and sprayed it into the caretaker's bucket you'd get an amazing buzz.

'I got a plan!' he announced later and I was worried in case he'd kill himself inhaling the spray.

'Chrissy, be careful. Yew could ruin yewer coat.'

'Don' give a toss, Siân,' was his only comment.

The following day, when he marked his name over half the desks during tutor period and was told to clean it off, I knew he meant business. When he never turned up for Maths second lesson, I feared the worst.

In the middle of boring bar-charts we heard the caretaker Mickey Brush giving off socks down the corridor. I pretended I had to go to the bogs as it was my time of the month and young Mr Delaney went beetroot instamatic.

What I witnessed was completely hilarious. Mickey was grappling with Chrissy, who had his head stuck in a bucket and wouldn't be shifted. When I nearly had a fit, Delaney couldn't stop Kar and Kerry rushing to the door to join me.

Kerry gawped at Chrissy, who screamed from inside the bucket.'Get off of me!'

'Y' dick!' Kerry said, 'I've yeard of a dope-ead, but never a bucket-ead!'

I thought Chrissy would be in real trouble for that, but all he got was a thousand lines on 'I must respect the caretaker's property'. If it had been Lloyd the Deputy's beloved garden bucket, he'd have been suspended.

Luckily there was a hole in it, so Chrissy didn't poison himself. He told us after that it had made him high, but nobody believed him. Kerry tried to explain what a real bucket was, but Chrissy ignored him. He preferred to listen to me. He even told other classes I was his half-sister. I think he always wanted a sister. Either that or he'd had one and been separated from her.

When Chrissy happened to mention to our form teacher Mrs. Jones, quite innocently, that Kerry was always on the bucket and they had the police up the school questioning him, Kerry decided to use me for his revenge. At first, I wasn't sure, then I thought of Shirley Egg and the good laugh we had and I agreed as long as Chrissy didn't get hurt.

I wanted to involve Gary Crissle cos I fancied him a bit, but he was lying low after Sparky's accident. In the end, I asked him not to grass us up to anyone in the Homes.

I managed to get Chrissy alone behind the mobiles on the long route to R.E., looking for someone with a fag.

'Chrissy,' I said casually, 'yew goin t' do this trolley race Friday?'

(Kerry and the boys had talked about it already, so I thought he'd have got wind.)

'Siân mun, yew know I'm opeless at sport. Got a fag by any chance?'

'Maybe ... it int sport exactly. It'll be a great larf!'

He was gasping and I could see he didn't want to get

involved. I used the bait and reeled him in easily.

'Yer, Chrissy, ave a fag ... Tell yew wha. If yew ave a go, I'll sponsor yew.'

'Sponsor? Yew takin-a piss?'

'No way! Yew jest gotta put my name on yewer trolley, tha's all.'

And that was it, he was well and truly in the net. I explained in detail what he had to do and Kerry's friend Jas did a professional poster advertising the event which we showed Chrissy. The only trouble was Chrissy could blab about it round the Homes and find it was a load of bull, so we told him it wasn't strictly legal and he had to keep his mouth shut.

Friday night soon came and we were all by the river near the fire-station as planned. A few of the other boys had nicked shopping-trolleys and put girls' names on them. Kerry had 'Shirley Egg' on his, of course. It did seem cruel, but I had a funny feeling Chrissy wouldn't turn up again and come up with one of his best-sellers as an excuse.

We finished our bottles of Hooch, but had to look out for cops cos we were right next to the college car-park where joy-riders practised hand-brake turns before roaring off for a burn. We'd timed it perfect, as crowds were making their drunken way over the bridge to the Cooler Club. Cwmtaff was a river in flood and we were the overspill.

Next thing, I could hear clapping and cheering and just make out Chrissy pushing a trolley with what resembled a Guy in it. He wheeled it down the path towards us, scattering clubbers. I was wrong about him. He was magnificent! For the first time ever, no trenchcoat. He wore swimming-goggles, a flappy, old-fashioned pilot's hat, leather jacket and black jeans. On the front of his trolley was 'SIAN GTi' in big red letters. Inside was a stuffed dummy with mop hair, meant to be me.

Me and Kar giggled like gibbons. We weren't being nasty.

'Reckon I could've found my best sport at last, eh Ker?' he told Kerry Richards. At that moment, I adored him. He'd put so much into my dummy, with its painted papier-mache head, bright lips outstanding.

'Penny f' the Siân?' he said, coming over to me and Kar. I was just about to put him off the whole thing in case he got humiliated, when Kerry took over.

'C'mon yew lot! Le's start before-a cops come an all-a crowds go away.'

He organized everything. It was a fix. They drew lots to go first, but Chrissy's was the only paper marked. He explained the rules for Chrissy's benefit and his gang smirked in the background. I wanted to speak out, but so far Chrissy had been the star.

He lined up by the riverside railings like Nigel Mansell ready to go. It was brill! He lowered his goggles and crashed into the metal. 'False start!' he shouted, grabbing the trolley and hauling it over the railings. It clattered onto the narrow bank and he followed, vaulting and showing off his talent. The second competitor, Dazzy, pushed his trolley up, making out he was prepared.

Chrissy launched his trolley through the air, down towards a small island of rocks and weeds in the Taff. My dummy jumped out and was soon floating downstream to the 'Ah's' of the crowd on the bridge. Chrissy leapt onto the weedy part of the island, showing tremendous agility. I thought he was going to swim after my dummy and retrieve it. Instead, he waved to the audience with his daft floppy hat and began to push his trolley in the general direction of Ponty. The river was fairly empty, as we'd had a few dry weeks, but still I was worried that he could be dragged down the weir ahead and end up seriously hurt cos of our sick joke.

The crowd were urging others to follow Chrissy. I joined in and Dazzy was beginning to regret it. I encouraged Chrissy as loud as I could, 'C'mon, Chrissy! Yew cun do it!'

'Siân! I always knew yew wuz a dummy!' said Kerry, cutting.

A police siren got rid of onlookers in seconds. Some of Kerry's gang went with them. Me, Kar and a few others ran along the river path, trying to keep sight of Chrissy. Karen was trying to get me to leave – 'Eh, Siân, we'd better leg it quick!', but followed me all the same.

The cops soon arrived. Four of them, one woman. Two men police went up to Kerry, who had a reputation, while the woman tackled us. She tried to be nice and also firm. The other cop shone his torch into the river.

'So what's goin on?' asked the WPC.

'F—in trolley race, carn yew see,' replied Kar, who was better than me at giving lip.

The WPC bristled and changed totally.

'Let's have less of your –'

She was cut off by a bloodcurdling cry from Chrissy. He must've reached the weir and fallen down it. All the cops ran in its direction, except the WPC. I could hear the tumble and crash of the trolley. One cop called 'Hey, come out of there!' as though Chrissy could stroll up the steep bank. I was surprised he didn't add 'Yew're trespassin!'

The WPC told us to clear off. We shoved past her and made for Chrissy's scream.

We stood by the footbridge to town and watched as three cops attempted to slide and scrape down the walls. One found the trolley, another slipped and floundered, while the third waded down the river. I wonder why they bothered when Cwmtaff was full of fights and joyriders.

Anyway, none of them caught Chrissy and we were driven home in a cop car. My mam was fuming cos we disturbed her bit of lovy-dovey on the sofa with her fancy man. She never cared what I did, as long as it wasn't the hard stuff. I'd be grounded for three months she said, but that was to impress the cops and her new boyfriend.

At school on Monday, there was no sign of Chrissy. I heard from Gary that the Homes had phoned the police reporting the stealing of girl's clothes and the disappearance of one Christian Evans.

Chrissy was a super hero. Kerry was as miffed as hell, and we decided to name the weir 'Chrissy's Leap'. When he returned to school later that week, he claimed he'd swum to Cardiff Docks and tried to board a boat to Jamaica disguised as a girl!

A week later, the dummy was fished out of the Taff by an aging angler who nearly had a heart-attack, thinking it was a dead body.

I asked Chrissy for a date, but he said he was still meeting Shirley Egg and, anyroad, what would people think if they saw him with his own half-sister?

Operation Slob

The only advantage of his house on Penôl estate was the view. From his room he could see towards the Beacons and across the valley to Abergwaun Mountain. A telescope was what he needed, but for the time being he made do with the binoculars his mam bought at a car-boot sale.

His life had improved since Mark Rees smashed himself up in an appropriate fashion. What was that Gary Crissle doing with him? It was a well known fact they loathed each other down to their soles. A case for investigation, but not by him.

He had more pressing matters.

Sparky had made his school hours a misery. Luckily, the boy was pretty thick so Matthew only had to endure him for certain subjects when they weren't setted. Most of his form worshipped him. How could they follow such a bully? No wonder Hitler had got to power.

'Yew're a mingin mong, Matt le Pissier!' he'd mocked, and his gestapo cronies had cackled.

'Better than a brainless dalek!' Matthew replied feebly.

'Yew wha?... Exterminate! Exterminate! Exterminate!' went Sparky endlessly round Matthew's desk, as they waited for the teacher to arrive. Jason Leigh thrust out a ruler like a dlaek's arm and prodded him. Others joined in, slapping him with rulers and chanting. He put his head down and tried to transmute into a Klingon. He concentrated hard. They pushed him from side to side. He slammed his hand down on his pencil case, reaching for his laser gun. Zap! Sparky gone!

And he had. Nobody surrounded Matthew. At the door, the Head of Year 8 Mr Protheroe glared at him. At Captain Matthew Setab (he preferred his surname backwards). Then the bell rang.

No it didn't. What he heard was his front door-bell. His mam was sleeping off her shift at B.O. Chocolates, so he'd have to be quick. He bounded down as it rang again: this time in code. Dee-dee dee-dah. *2001 Space Odyssey.* Engineer Carl Seivad at just the right moment.

Carl was a gangling boy with big, blue eyes who was in the Special Class. He had a cosmic imagination, but couldn't write it down. He could speak fluent Vulcan, but never answer a question in class. He could decipher the code of their Starship Urinal, but found full-stops and commas impossible.

Matthew opened the door.

'Yew called O Captain?' Carl greeted him and entered the hall, limbs moving in all directions at once.

'Remarkable!' said Matthew, leading his friend upstairs, 'yewer powers of telepathy are extraordinree.'

In his room, Carl settled comfortably on the bed, while Matthew paced up and down, staring out the window occasionally. He tried not to glance at Carl's legs, oddly open as he sat. He focussed on his father in that wardrobe in his mam's bedroom. The room he'd never enter. His dead father's clothes still hanging there. Terrestial and trivial preoccupations. There was no heaven, only space. Above and around. For them.

'Take a look at 'is, Captain.' Carl held out a scrap of paper with what looked like maths formula on. 'I've already decoded it.'

'Okay ... what's it mean?' He halted and faced Carl, squinting to avoid looking down.

'Yew were right. It's a bit o' Kerry's work an it's in Martian.'

Matthew chuckled and stroked his chin

'Thought so. No ewman could take all them pills an still end up gettin 80% for maths. Them chemicals must be essential for is survival.'

'Wha shall we do?'

Matthew gazed out of his window for inspiration.

'I know! ... we'll activate the Starship, do a scannin orbit round Mars an pick up info on Richards ... '

'Is Martian name's Slob, it says on yer.'

'Mmm ... that figures. I'm tol the Martians are a bit like the Red Indians in that respect.'

'Eh?'

'Well, they're called accordin to theyr character like... Right,' he touched Carl's shoulder gently. 'Le's go!'

He stepped gingerly out, wary not to wake his mam. Carl clodhopped and creaked the floorboards. He heard his mam turn and stir, but no shout came. He pressed the switch outside the bathroom several times, then whispered into the key-hole the code-word 'Bogalactic'.

Captain Setab pushed open the hatch door. Engineer Seivad took up his post on the toilet-seat, after sealing and locking the hatch. He held both taps and looked into the mirror.

'Check energy levels, Engineer Seivad!' Seivad turned the shower on and a spray burst out, wetting the arm of his jumper.

'Sod it! ... energy levels 100%.'

'Check fuel!'

Seivad flushed the toilet vigorously and during the water's rush said, 'Fuel tank's full, Captain.'

'Right! All systems go! Operation Slob is under way!'

Captain Setab turned the taps on and off, peering ahead at his reflection in the mirror over the sink. Seivad did the countdown into the shower-head, interrupted by a gurgle of water before he declared 'Take off!'

Starship Urinal was on its way through space. Its captain skillfully negotiating the route past meteors and avoiding next-door's satellite dish. The Engineer now looked into the scanner.

'There's a strange mist ahead, Captain.'

'It's the Sea of Condensation ... a weird gas close to Mars. We'll ave t' ewse lasers to smash ower way through.'

Seivad stretched the shower hose towards the mirror and aimed.

'Lasers ready, sir.'

'Right! Fire!'

Seivad attempted to turn on the bath tap operating the shower and a spurt of water missed the mirror, hitting Captain Setab straight in the face. He should've been obliterated.

'Yew bloody idiot! Lucky it wuz on'y a test run. Now get it right next time!'

'Yew aim the lasers. I carn do both,' Carl grinned.

The Sea of Condensation was destroyed and they rapidly approached Mars itself. Protector shields were essential, so Seivad drew across the shower-curtain.

'I've located theyr main HQ. All I need t' do is ome in on theyr computers. I'm shewer I cun ack them easy.'

Carl heard footsteps on the landing. Matthew was too busy adjusting the toothbrush computer terminals.

'Sir, aliens approaching on warp 19!'

'Don't be darft ...!'

His mam knocked and tried the handle.

'Yew in there, Matthew? I'm bustin! Urry up!'

'Oh no!' She normally slept all morning. It was the first time she'd disturbed them and the window was too small for an emergency exit and space-walk down to the back-yard.

'Wha now, Matthew?' Carl seemed gormless – a real rem, he thought.

'What yew doin, Matthew?'

Matthew's brain whirred, wanting to find some Vulcan logic.

'Carl's in yer, mam ... ee felt bard ... ee wuz sick ... I'm elpin im.'

The two nodded, took deep breaths and decided to do a crash-landing back on earth. Setab unsealed the hatch door. In her cosy, yellow night-gown, the puffy-eyed alien blinked at the boys. Carl hung his head, acting ill.

'Hiya, Mrs Bates,' he groaned.

'Sorry, mam!'

She shoved past them, mumbling, 'I don' know. I jest don' know. I wonder wha yewer dad woulda said.'

Starship Urinal had been attacked by a storm of mete-orites. It was undergoing reconstruction at Cape Penôl. Setab and Seivad planned to complete Operation Slob another day.

That night, however, Matthew saw something much more interesting through his binoculars. From his bed-room-observatory he spotted a beam of light on the hori-zon. He'd pointlessly traced many planes, but this was different. It dipped, spun, glowed and appeared to land at the exact place where a large gas-tank was situated, in countryside near Laverstayne's Hotel.

He waited a long time for the light to rise, but it never did. Could the gas-tank be connected to some operation?

He remembered Richards' dad. He had to tell Carl, but his friend wasn't allowed out on Sundays. His parents were very holy and talked in tongues. So, on Monday, he'd have to impress on his friend how they must act quickly before Slob and his kind took over. Matthew could see him replacing Sparky as his main tormentor.

He caught hold of Carl as he was coming out of Bob 'the dog' Jones's Maths lesson. 'Le's go to the bogs down yer.'

It was an OUT day and most pupils would soon be shunted along the corridors. There was a chance of peace in the toilet.

As always, the corridor was a stampede from Games to the Hall for food. They were Year 7's and Matthew pushed them out of his way.

'This is no place for a genius.'

'I don' see one anyway,' replied Carl, dodging bodies, 'so wha's up?'

'Vital info,' Matthew whispered, raising his voice as they entered the sewer-stench, 'it's Kerry Richards. I've discovered....'

Both stood shock-still. It wasn't coincidence. His words had come alive. In front of them was Richards, with his trainer-top hood up, involved in a shady deal with a boy he didn't recognise. He was about to scat, when Kerry saw them, stung by his uttered name. He hid something in a pocket and approached. The other rummaged in his bag, jerking his head at them. Kerry practically stood on Matthew's toes. The other boy took out a blade and came up behind him, slapping the knife on his palm.

'Put tha away and check the door. I'll sort 'is one, Way....' he checked himself. 'Orright! Yew grass us up an

I'll tell ev'ryone I seen yew two in yer together doin revoltin thin's. Right?'

Matthew and Carl both nodded meekly.

'No problem, Kerry,' Carl said.

'Teacher! Quick!' the other shouted and he and Kerry disappeared into the cubicles. Matthew and Carl left just as sharply, down the corridor away from the teacher on duty. They tried to walk calmly, though Matthew's legs wobbled and stomach churned.

At a quiet spot near the Games Hall, they breathed deeply and Matthew began to explain about the light.

'I jest put two an two together....'

'Tha's more 'an I cun do.'

'Listen ... my theory is tha Richards is meetin is fellow Martians up-a gas-tank. Is dad works there, I know fer a fact.'

'I know I'm slow but ... wha do Martians wan' gas-tanks for?'

'Look, I seen-a light. It wuz definitely a U.F.O. P'raps 'ey need gas f' power, I dunno. We gotta follow it up even if Slob isn't be'ind it ... . I got a plan. This Friday night it's gunna be fine – accordin t' the forecast. We need saws, combat gear ... er, a polaroid camera or cam-corder. . . .'

'Ow we gunna get tha lot?'

'My dad ad saws, no prob. Combat gear ... um. . . find out two boys oo go t' the cadets.'

'What shell I tell em?'

'Say we need it fer a Fancy Dress party. My mam's got a polaroid, so tha's okay. Yew've got a week t' get the equipment. Okay, Engineer Seivad?'

'Aye ... Captain. What the ell d' we need a saw for? Choppin off Martians' antennae as evidence or wha?'

'Yew'll see. Got it from 'Macbeth', din I? Ol Shakey's good for summin.'

'Yew're bloody loop-the-loop, yew know wha!'

All that week Matthew reassured Richards he had no intention of telling on him. He also asked about the gas-tank in an off-hand way, which confirmed Richards' belief that Matthew was crazy beyond help.

Carl was soon successful in borrowing army clothes. He made up a story about a party up the Youth and the boys who lent him the gear said they might gatecrash it, which would lead to more lies later.

Everything was falling into place. Friday would bring the answer.

'Ow d' we get up there?' Carl asked during tutor period that day.

'Bus, then walk. We're visitin friends up Beacon Park.'

'But I don' know no-one there.'

'No, nerd features. Anyone sees us, tha's what we tell em. By the way, yew'll need a tidy rucksack f' the gear.'

'I gotta be back by arf-ten, or my parents'll kill me.'

'Resurrection is another o' my specialities! ... Look, tell em a story, say yew woz kidnapped by aliens or summin. Blame it on me. Say we wuz lost.'

All that day Carl was wound up. Whenever he saw Matthew he checked about the time and equipment and should he bring green face-paint. Matthew eventually got exasperated and told him to 'Shut it!' He had a strange feeling that Richards was observing their manic behaviour.

He had planned the bus times, allowing plenty of leeway. He'd had a job finding out. Hardly any ran after 6 p.m. and as it was the route to Abergwaun, it was naturally Pontypridd Bus Co. that ran it! Such illogicality would drive a Vulcan to suicide.

It was half-ten and Carl's home-time when they were getting off at the entrance to Beacon Park, a new estate on the Nedd Road. The weather was different to town: a thick mist and it was chilly. The bus-driver (seeing the rucksacks) told them they wanted the Beacons not Beacon Park and Carl blurted, 'Sokay, we're untin fer aliens!' The driver laughed. Matthew nudged his friend. The bus left and Carl looked at his watch.

'Don' worry. I'll make shewer we get lost.'

Carl sniggered anxiously, jogging on the spot to keep warm. Matthew gazed round and saw the bus-shelter opposite.

'Right, Seivad, over the road t' get togged out. Operation Gas-tank is now under way!'

'It's a pity we couldn 've brung yewr bathroom with us. I feel safer in there.'

'Ne' mind, tha bus wuz like a toilet on wheels. What more d' yew wan'?'

As cars and lorries sped past, they changed in the shelter. Engineer Seivad was now more eager to venture into the unknown.

'Leave the balaclavas an face-paints. Le's go an cut down a couple o' trees.'

Despite the mist, their torches found the track used by motorbikes across slag-heaps past Beacon Park. Matthew had seen it many times from his dad's car on the way to Swansea. He'd been a disappointment to his dad, but this was more in his line, physical and manly.

Seivad nattered loudly, making out he wasn't afraid. He strode in front till a rush of noise (actually a lorry) made him clutch Setab like a toddler scared of the dark. A large white owl flew across their path and over the moors. It was magical. Setab could believe he was already on another planet.

When the track ended they clambered over a hillock. They could see the lights of Laverstayne's by the side of the main road. The gas-tank had a wall of mist behind it.

They soon came to a small plantation of conifers, most not tall enough for camouflage.

'Birnam Wood hath been shrunk.'

'Eh? ... What we gunna do?'

'I think there's more near the otel. We'll afto risk it.'

On the next rise of ground, Setab took out his binoculars and surveyed the scene.

'Carn I ave a go?'

'In a moment, Seivad. I've located the alien spy-station. There are larger trees further on. Birnam shall come to Laverstayne.'

'Yew don' ave t' talk in Martian, y' know.'

Carl thwacked his friend's rucksack, sending him toppling.

'I'll ave yew court-martialed....' Matthew righted himself.

'C'mon! Give me a go!'

'Okay! But no messin.'

Setab led the way, asserting his authority. Seivad kept stopping to try out the binoculars. In a slight hollow, not far from the main road, he startled his Captain.

'I seen summin! Certain! 'ave a look!'

Setab moon-hopped back. He picked up on a beam above the gas-tank, which was descending. There was a bright glow and then, suddenly, the whole thing went dark. At the same time, he could've sworn he heard a weird whining.

'Did yew see it?' Seivad's eyes bulged so he looked like the alien.

'I did. Tha's it! Same as las Saturday. The UFO. An I yeard summin.'

'So did I! Think we oughta go on? Maybe we should tell-a cops.'

'I'm surprised at yew, Engineer. Our mission's on'y started an we aven even got lost yet.'

'Aye, orright. But I'm goin straight inta the otel if there's trouble.'

'Maybe the aliens 're stayin there. No-one else would!'

They continued with the mission, crossing the road and nearing the hotel. Matthew recalled the one time he'd been there as a treat, to celebrate his parents fifteenth anniversary, before his dad got really sick. It was a disaster: brickhard scampi and his dad had veal which he called 'gone-off gammon'.

Past the hotel, they ducked into the forestry and got out the saws. They greened their faces and grinned crescents that weren't to be seen in the sky.

'Maybe they'll accept us as brothers.'

'What d' yew reckon theyr ship's like?'

'Carn beat the Starship Urinal, I'd say.'

'I ope theyr friendly.'

'Like Slob?'

'I don' think ee....'

'Okay. Le's get 'ese trees cut!'

With hacksaws they found it tough. Setab's hands were sore and he wished he'd worn gloves. Seivad clasped his tree so firmly, he uprooted it. Setab couldn't do the same, so they both held tight onto a smaller one and eventually yanked it out.

With green faces, balaclavas, combat gear and holding trees in front of them, they looked like poor imitators of 'Who Dares Wins' not UFO fiends. Further into the forestry, Setab was lost. The conifers were looming and he couldn't see the tank.

'Bearins, Engineer?'

'Somewhere west o' Jupiter, Captain.'

'Don' take the piss. I'm serious. We're bloody lost!'

'Oh well, at least I won' ave t' lie t' my parents.'

'At this rate....'

'Why don' we jest turn back?'

Setab took out the binoculars. Trees, trees and more trees, but he could make out a forest track and told Seivad, persuading him to give it one last chance. When they reached it, he picked up fresh tyre-marks in his torchlight.

'The Slobmobile! We're on the right track at last!'

Carl dragged along reluctantly. He was quiet now, worrying about excuses. Matthew ploughed on, aiming his beam ahead.

A car!

'Get down! Quick!'

'Wha?'

They crouched behind the trees.

'There's a car a'ead. I bet it's the Richards. I reckon the tank's really close.'

'So where's the ship?'

'Dunno, but I'm gunna get some proof. Keep an eye on me an get ready t' run.'

He left his stuff with Seivad and crawled along a ditch. Too many twigs snapped, so he returned to the track and stooped, prowling like a cat, shining his beam along the ditch for direction. His heart beat so loud it seemed to echo for miles. He was terrified and excited in one. He heard moaning.

Was it an alien spying from the trees? He thought of retreating, but Seivad would desert him forever if he did.

He shone on the number-plate. The moaning was coming from the car. It got louder and louder: two voices one upon the other. He raised the polaroid. He crabbed his way around under the car windows. The moans ceased. There were whispers. He jumped up and aimed. In the flash he glimpsed a tangle of flesh.

'What the f—in ell's goin on?'

'Oh my God, Col! Private dicks!'

Matthew turned and fled. The car-door was flung open and a stout man came out, pulling up his trousers and doing his zip.

'Ey, I'll ave yew! Yew dirty bleeder!'

Carl saw all this through the binoculars and was already making a dash when Matthew caught up with him. Matthew swung the camera strap round his head and it hit a jutting branch.

The heavily-built man pursued them but didn't get far. His previous exertions took their toll. He also realised he was in his socks when he trod on a cone and cursed. He hopped back to his car, started it, driving down the bumpy track. By then, the boys had veered off and lay panting, willing to stay till morning.

'Richards?' Carl asked.

'Well if it woz then is wife int goin t' be too pleased.'

'Shell we go an find-a spaceship 'en?'

'Yew're great yew are! Now yew're interested! Arfta all tha! No way, Carl. I've ad enough f' one night!'

They took ages to get home, but Matthew's mam was still in bed after her shift. A police-car had stopped them and asked their names. Matthew had explained they were in the Army cadets and had lost their way. The police were easily convinced by their appearance.

The next night Matthew again used binoculars to

search for the UFO across valley. No beam. No glow. Nothing. Perhaps they'd frightened them off? And that couple having sex there as well. They wouldn't return.

He'd replaced the camera in its drawer under the stairs. There was no sign of the photo though. He felt sure his dad would've been proud of his resourcefulness. He'd never make a private detective, but as an alien-hunter he'd made a start. Monday would bring Slob and that Martian cunning still had to be dealt with.

Eco Terror Hits Blaenmorlais !!!

I'm standing on top of the bus-shelter in Blaenmorlais and all the kids are cackling at me like hens on a spree. I've only got underpants on and I want to fly away.

I flap my arms furiously, but nothing happens. I turn to see a strange sluggish smoke creeping across the astro-turf and through the houses towards us. I hop up and down cos the roof's burning my feet. The mustard-coloured stuff is nearing. The grinning faces of my friends are covered and choked by the smoke below me. They're lost in its deadly smog and I'm king-of-the-castle, above it all. A fiercesome growl and a snow-plough thing comes downhill, shoving aside the smog and also the kids with it. They're gone! It brakes and I jump down. I want to run, but there's a wind I can't hear stopping me. A demolition ball is hurtling towards me, being controlled by the vehicle. In the cab I just make out the face of my step-father, Colin, loving every moment, tugging the lever. Like a 3D film. On an escalator the wrong way. Naked and frail. The metal ball hits my head. I fall flat, hit the pavement. Blood! Sweat! I'm drenched. Like when I used to wet the bed. My mam's calling for me to get up.

'Winston Williams! 'urry up!'

She always does that. My full name, same as registration.

'Oh shit!'

The dream still hangs over me. My childish Postman Pat lampshade.

'The bastard! The f—in twat!'

Colin appears at my door, as I roll over from thumping the pillow.

'Winston? Are yew f—in talkin t' yewer mam like tha?'

'No, it's yew.... I mean ... I carn elp it!'

'Don' talk bull an if yew don' get up sharpish, I'll make yew bloody elp it!'

White vest, hairy chest. Where was his medallion? I hate my name. The kids call me 'Winny' or even 'the Poo' which is worse. I'd have liked to spell it 'Winstone' after that boxer who owned the café down town.

Colin leaves me to my thoughts of the dream and its meaning. My mates wouldn't laugh at me like that. And Colin, that's the sort of thing he'd do. Wish I could've driven that snow-plough. If only you could script dreams like the videos we made with Doc Stewart once. He was ace and I used to take the piss out of his posh accent. He never minded if you swore in lessons as long as it wasn't at him. He was the only one who appreciated my disease. I saw a documentary about it on telly, this boy couldn't stop swearing and all the doctors reckoned it was an illness, Baron Richthoven's Syndrome or something.

Doc was a hero cos he got me promoted. See, I was in the Specials before I went up his class to be interviewed by my friend Gavin Williams. There's nothing special about the Specials. If you ask me, it's a fancy way of calling us Rems. It was frustrating cos some teachers thought we were all thick and not worth bothering with. Not Doc though.

I was allowed out to be interviewed about Rudge's plant in Blaenmorlais, near where I live. Gav asked me questions like 'What are the effects of Rudge's on the community of Blaenmorlais?' And I replied 'F—in disastrous. Like a bleedin plague.'

When Doc read it after, he pointed out that the bad language would have to be edited out for the class magazine they were doing. Otherwise, he said it was great and asked me to jot down my opinions on Rudge's. He told me – never mind the lack of full-stops – that I could be a good journalist. I could've sprouted wings there and then and soared like a hawk.

Next thing I knew, I was on trial in the proper English class and sitting by Gav. Don't ask me how Doc wangled it, with his torn trousers and boots fit for a skinhead. But this year it's 'Terror' Thomson and all my work's covered in red. If I had a nose-bleed over it, you wouldn't notice! He mostly does boring exercises with dictionaries. I liked Doc's lessons on the environment. If the world's going to end it won't be a war, it'll be a slow strangling of the planet. Rudge's are part of it, but what can we do? That smog in my dream was telling me something.

On the day of that dream, I have a whizzbanger barney with Mrs Joyce, our Geog teacher. She makes me feel a tiny grub cos I covered a map of the world all over in blue felt-tip.

'And what do you call this, Winston Williams?' There you go again, full name. Why me? She sounds posher than Doc now, who never talks down.

'The f ... er ... the sea miss?'

I'm proud of my self-control.

'So the sea covers all the world, does it? That's news to me! You're a waste of space and you can do this properly during break.'

'Yew wait,' I mutter.

44

'Sorry, Winston, did you say something?'

'No miss.' I whisper to Gavin, 'I'll show er!' so he knows I mean it.

At breaktime, I go half way. I put in her cities and find out which are the low lands next to oceans. I cover them in blue instead.

Kerry Richards sticks his head into the classroom and chants 'Naughty boy, naughty boy, naughty boy!' Then I hear Joggy Joyce highpitching at him. She sits next to me clutching her mug of tea. She lifts up my map as if its full of germs. She tries to stay calm.

'Much better, Winston, but still too blue. Are you by any chance an Everton fan?'

'Yew wha miss?' She probably knows more about football than me.

'Look, I'm sorry, but I must insist on it being done properly at home. Do you understand?'

It's too much. Like a big blow to my skull.

'I ope yew move t' Olland miss. F—in global f—in warmin tha's wha it's about, not bleedin Everton.'

She stammers in disbelief then sends me to the Head of Year, Mrs Watkins, who gives me a long lecture in her office, which is full of the delicious smell of filter coffee. I'm sniffing and she thinks I'm about to start blubbering.

'One more time and yew'll be suspended. There's no excuse for ewsing bard language to a teacher like that! I want it to stop! Do yew yer me Winston?'

How is it teachers always say 'Do you hear me?' when they're two feet away and breaking the sound barrier? Do they think we're all Heavy Metal fans suffering from too much head-banging?

'Carn elp it miss. I got 'is disease, see. It's serious.'

'But yew're ardly ever off school, I know for a fact....'

'No miss. Baron Richthoven's Syndrome. It makes yew swear all-a time. I seen this film....'

'The disease yew've got is lyin, not swearin!'

The phone rings and I stand like a punch-bag. Mrs Watkins is in deep conversation. I hear 'Mrs Connell' mentioned so it must be about Liam. I wonder what it could be cos Liam's in school for once. When she finally puts the phone down, she seems to have forgotten our conversation and makes a general threat.

'Any more trouble er ... Winston ... and I'll ave yewr parents up yer. Right?'

'Okay, miss!'

Later that day on telly there's an item about these Eco-warriors climbing trees to protect an area. Colin's socks pose a greater threat than opencast coal, his feet up on the coffee-table. He blows smoke-rings across my vision and fingers *The Sun* for smut. I wish I could turn into that insect I was made to feel earlier by Joggy. I'd climb one of his socks and it'd be worse than Rudge's tip. I'd give him such a nip. I must've said something without realising it.

'What yew on about, Win? Int yew goin out? Yew carn stand *Neighbours*, s' yew might as well.'

The doorbell rings and Colin springs up. Not like him. Usually, you'd need a crane to shift him. He's on the dole and dosses around a lot. Most people search for jobs, but not him with his suspicious activities. One of these arrived now in the form of Dessie Drew, carrying a old hold-all. Dessie took one look at me and was off.

'Winston mun! Yewr ol man shoulda called yew Mike or summin. That way yew'd be able t' spell it, eh?'

He sneers and winks at Colin, who wants me out.

'Look, Win. Go an buy yewrself some chips, there's a good lad. Me an Dessie gotta discuss business.'

He thrusts a fiver into my hand. A fiver! All of a sudden so generous!

'Ta! I'll get f—in scampi an chips fer tha. ... Carn I join yewr business, dad?' I say it so sarky, if Dessie hadn't been there, Colin would've lumped me.

'Off yew go ... an don' tell yewr mam, right?'

He points his thumb at the door like a hitchhiker. As I'm leaving Dessie makes out to punch me but scruffles my hair. I jerk back in a nervous twitch.

'See yewr language aven improved, Winston boy!'

It's great to get out. I dash up the chippie, hearing the noise of machinery from Rudge's. I can never get used to it.

It's a big hole filled with rubbish and God knows what. Two weeks ago one of their lorries spilled its load onto the High St. The cops and Environmental Health were there. It was black stuff like tar, only smelt worse than our school bogs. In the local paper Rudge's claimed it was harmless. All I know is, the road still has a burnt patch.

I skirt the astroturf football pitch. My mam's told me the Opencast built it as a reward for people putting up with seventeen years of dust, rats and racket. Perfect place: when the wind takes fumes from Rudge's the players can come off feeling a lot less fit and wheezing. My mam hates it, but prefers it to the Opencast cos at least it doesn't spoil her washing. I explained that it was only cos she couldn't actually see the pollution so easily.

I hold the fiver and feel like a lottery winner. Can't wait to get rid of it, as it might be dirty money. At Sam the Chippie's, the woman doesn't rip it to check. I order scampi and chips, a Mars and four cans of shandy in a carrier. These are for my friends Gav, Twti and Leggo. They'd be amazed at my generosity.

Twti and Leggo both go to St. Kevin's. Twti had once been small but isn't any more and Leggo does have long legs, but that doesn't account for his nickname. His real name's Darren Legg, see.

When I reach the bench up the Gardens, a small area of green opposite the Burger Palace, where we usually meet, Leggo's the only one absent. Sometimes he has trouble getting out. His parents are strict and check his homework.

Gav's entertaining the others with impressions of teachers. He's great at the RE teacher Dafto Davies and does his booming voice perfect.

'Now then 9Z! One of each gender next to each other! You by there with the elephant ears! This is a school not a zoo!'

'Orright boys, it's Christmas!' I fling them a can each and tuck into the scampi. They pick at my chips like precinct pigeons, leaving the shandy till later.

'Ey, Winny! Yew bin nickin yewr dad's money agen?'

'Listen! Ee int my dad an I got the money tidy. Well, bit o' bribery like.'

Soon Leggo turns up looking sheepish. Gav lays into him, smoothing his hair.

'All yewer work done, Darren darlin?'

'Give over!' Leggo swipes at him, catches a chip I'm going to eat and sends it flying into the flower-bed.

'Right Leggo, yew don get yewr pressie now boy!'

I make him jump for the can, like a dog doing tricks.

On the way up the Blaen's steep hill I'd been thinking. I had to exorcise that dream like a demon. I hoped the boys would co-operate. As soon as they got bored, I'd make my point.

'Le's go up Pwll Park fera bit o' action, is it?' suggested Leggo, trying to improve his image.

'Na! I yeard 'ere's a f—in disco up Pwll Club an evr'yone's goin there,' I lie, 'why don' we go down-a bus-shelter, eh? Mandy an em could be down 'ere. I could ewse-a rest o' my bribe t' f—in bribe er.'

'Wouldn go with er,' says Twti, 'don' know where she've bin. Yew could catch summin f—in serious.'

Leggo isn't convinced by my story, but since I've given them the shandy, they feel they owe me one. We end up in the shelter and I have to act fast before they get fed up again. I ask Gav to give me a leg up and haul myself onto the roof. He's about to follow, so I start a speech to get their attention.

'If I ad a pair o' dirty Y-fronts I'd set fire to em! Ladies an ... shitty little subewmans!'

'Ey, watch it!' pipes Twti, protecting his nickname.

'I'd like yew t' raise yewr cans in tribute to ower sponsor. Tha great bleedin w—r isself ... the Baron Richthoven!'

To cries of 'Ee's mad!' and 'Yew mus be trippin!' I raise my can and shake it viciously. I hold it between my legs, open it and spray them like a gone-wrong Grand Prix victor. They do the same, yelping and yapping, as I try to catch their fountains in my mouth.

I take a long last swig. Over the astroturf there's a low fog. Down the road comes a bright green Beetle, which nearly hits Leggo as he lurches into the road. It halts downhill and reverses. I get down in case – the cops take all shapes nowadays. I half expect to see Colin as the window's wound down.

There are two men in the car. Early 20's I'd say. Look like students. Leggo backs off, while me and Gav approach thinking they want directions. Twti swigs and pretends to be cool.

'Hey, lads!' the passenger, with a pony-tail, speaks, 'is Rudge's anywhere round here?'

I notice a Greenpeace sticker on one window and warm to them.

'Yeh, over by there!' I point past our row of terraces, towards the dark. 'But the main entrance is off-a slip-road back there by-a Palace. Bit late fera visit, in it?'

'No, we're just here to monitor the situation. Speak to the locals. That sort of thing.... What do you think of it?'

Gav acts hard, 'Couldn give a shit!'

'They're jest ruinin people's lives,' I butt in, 'ey don' give a toss 'bout us. I'd like t' put a bomb under it personally. They're a load o' f—ers!'

They aren't shocked. The driver nods away and the other smiles.

'Yeh, you could be right. Anyway, thanks for your time. We'll see you round maybe?'

'Aye!'

They drive off towards town. I turn to Gav.

'S' ow come yew done tha interview, when yew don' give a shit?'

'It woz a project. We ad to do summin. I knew yew'd elp so....'

'Oo woz 'ey anyway?' asks Twti.

'Bloody English, tha's all I know!' says Leggo, even though his mam's from London.

'Greenpeace, I bet. Didn yew see-a sticker? Someone's gunna do summin 'bout Rudge's an about time too.'

'What'll 'ey do? Launch a loada ships onta Top Pond,

is it?' Gav cuts.

'Anyway, my dad works there an ee says it's orright. It's bloody jobs an there's ardly any round yer, is there?'

'Yew make me sick, Leggo! If 'ey put a f—in newclear plant by-a Palace yew'd say-a same!'

'I know loadsa kids got asthma!' says Twti, carried by my anger.

'Well Rudge's int exactly Churnobull, is it?' argues Gav, not giving in. He'd done his project and not believed a word. He might even have done it to get me into his set.

'S' yewr project woz bullshit?'

'No, but....'

Mandy Hopkins breaks off his sentence with a shout from across the road, 'ey boys!' She comes over with Karen Bennett, who usually bothers with Siân Jones. Mandy's got a skirt on her like a serviette. Karen has lipstick bright as the Burger Palace lights.

'Any fags boys?' asks Mand. I'm not letting Gav go that easy, he's on the ropes.

'They got drums o' chemicals there, Gav, I know fera fact. They're burnin up all kinda shit. It's f—in lethal!'

But he was too busy eyeballing the girls. Leggo was handing out the fags. Everyone ignored me.

'Why int yew up-a disco in Pwll?' Gav asks them.

'What disco? There int one!' says Karen.

Gavin gives me a glare. He puffs out smoke while Leggo and Twti chat up Karen, who inhales like a spliff. I just want to get away, to sort my head.

'I'm off, boys. S'long!' They chorus replies and only Gavin shouts out 'Wha's up, Winny?' after me. I walk towards home, peering back to see them disappear into the shelter. Their laughter flocks together and I feel lonely. I can't go in. My mam would be back from her shift and her and Colin would either be bonking away or he'd be out somewhere and she'd be watching telly. She'd be miserable, wouldn't talk, worrying what he was up to. The bonking was worse mind.

I slept with earphones on and woke with a stiff neck. That's not all that was stiff either!

I pass my house and head for the gate to the astroturf. What does my mam see in Colin? He's a slob! She left my real dad when I was small. He had a mental problem. For all I know he still has and is wandering the streets of Cardiff or stuck in a hospital.

I'm surprised to find the gate open. I squeeze my way in and feel like a burglar. It's a starless night with drizzle in the air. Nobody's around here. I go and sit on a small wooden stand and hunch myself up like a hedgehog. I'm still cold and punch the air, an out-of-place boxer on the touchline. The mist's lurking, but I spot headlights searching down our street and hide behind the changing-rooms. Hope it isn't the caretaker come to lock up.

The car turns into the rough drive to the gate. I can see it's that bright green VW. They park before the gate and two doors open. I back off, as I could be seen in the beam. I sit, back to the changing-rooms, gazing over at Rudge's, fence in the distance topped with barbed-wire. My bum's sopping like I'd pissed myself. I'm on pins.

Whispers louden as they approach: two English accents and another, definitely Cwmtaff. I think maybe they've spied me and nearly shit myself, till they open the changing-room door and enter.

'All the gear's here. You two get changed.'

'Ow the ell did yew sort this out?'

It's unmistakably Colin! I can't believe it! Colin, a secret member of Greenpeace and on a vital mission? But they wouldn't hire crooks, that's for certain. It doesn't figure.

'I'll go back to the car and keep look-out.'

'Fine!'

'Ey, this is like-a bleedin SAS, in it?'

One leaves and shuts the door. Now the conversations are muffled and I hear the thump and clatter of their actions, under torchlight I suppose.

No sign of Dessie Drew or battered hold-alls. What they are up to would be risky, with the security at Rudge's, dogs and alarms. The door re-opens and this time Colin sounds serious.

'Further on up! Away from-a ouses!'

I swallow big gulps of air. They run past rapidly, two shapes in camouflage and balaclavas. Colin was right: the SAS. One carries a hold-all, could be Dessie's. No stolen videos after all, unless they're going to flog them to the security-guards!

I daren't move till they're well away and at the fence. I bum-shuffle slowly from behind the changing-rooms. Not much cover, but if I can get to the fence further on. ... I glimpse them clipping the wire.

It's late and I'm tired. It's like a film I'm scripting, except for one mis-cast character: I should be out there, not Colin.

Soon they're through the fence and not a bark from the dogs. It's weird! One catches his trousers on a jag of wire and swears 'Oh f—k!' That's Colin alright. I'd look for evidence later.

By the time I've crabbed to the fence, I'm so soaked I cease to care. My hands are scrabbed by thistles and weeds. I lie in wait and breathe deep. Rudge's sounds unusually silent. I expect a bell to ring out or even an explosion.

I become drowsy despite having the shivers. A furious barking makes me wide awake. Running feet. Colin and the man squeeze through the gap. Colin catches his sleeve this time, the dozy bugger. He tugs and a piece comes off.

The dog isn't getting nearer, which is odd. But in case, I crawl back to the relative safety of the changing-rooms.

Car doors open. Lights on. Reaching me. I drop face down.

They reverse with a screech like a car-chase in a film. Soon as the lights point away, I hide by the cabin (used for the office). They drive past our house and into the High Street.

Open ground in front of me. If the guard comes near, I'd be sniffed out.

My back to the cabin like a firing-squad. Alsatian's barking sounds closer now, perhaps by the gap. Just as I'm going to leg it, the noise fades. Saved! Motionless a while, my palms sting and my jeans are drenched.

I run home hoping my mam's still up. No lights had come on for the car or dog, it's that late. I press our bell again and again. Through the glass square I see the kitchen striplight flicker on. Someone comes from the back. Opens up.

It's Colin, looking flustered.

'Where-a f—in ell yew bin?'

We eye each other up and down like a couple of fight- ers weighing in. I fist my hands to conceal scratches. He's wearing T-shirt and jeans. No marks on his arm, but one leg of his jeans are torn. He's got cat's eyes, prowling.

'Wi' my friends, up Top Pond.'

'Wha? Bit late f' skinny-dippin, in it?... I ope yew int in no trouble?'

'Yew wha?... yew're a fine one....'

'Oi! Less o' that!' He sounds like he's off *Eastenders*. 'I'm off up anyway.'

I'd love to accidentally burst into the bathroom, to see if he's tending a cut, but I've got enough evidence anyway. I go to my room and undress quietly as possible. Don't want to wake my sister Charlene, who'd bawl and claim I'd done it on purpose. I wipe myself drier with a shirt from the floor, yesterday's washing.

In the distance, a police siren. It could be going to Rudge's. I can't sleep, my mind whirling about Colin and Greenpeace. Only the once had he given his view on the plant: 'I wouldn work there if yew paid me!' My mam sensibly replied: 'Yew wouldn work anywhere if they paid yew.' I should've examined the fence and taken any cloth, to be certain. It's too dangerous to return and might be teeming with cops.

In the morning there's no sign of Colin. And by the time I get home that evening the Blaen is buzzing with rumours. My mam's back early from work and getting tea, while Char is pestering me as usual.

'Pooh bear! Stinky poo!' she grabs my trousers.

'Get off, yew boggin pain!' I shake her off and she goes crying to mam.

'Leave er be, Winston!'

'Yer mam ! Yeard about the break-in at Rudge's?'

'Aye! They done a fair bit o' damage apparently, but nothin wuz stolen.'

Char won't give in and screams, 'Int yew gunna it im, mam?'

'Give over now, Char! ... I think they musta bin scared off. ... Yew don' know nothin, d' yew?'

I wonder what Colin might've said about last night.

On cue, he enters the house. Char forgets her upset and launches herself at him. Her dad. I go for it. The count-down.

'Ey Colin! What d' yew think about tha f—in break-in up Rudge's? Reckon it wuz locals?'

He doesn't respond, mumbles 'Dunno!' and plonks a large Argos bag on the kitchen table.

'Christmas is early this year!' he announces, as Char dives in with a gleeful yell, pulling out a box which turns out to be a remote-controlled car. My mam laughs more heartily than for years.

'What yew get er tha for? I swear yew wanted a son!'

'Maybe it's for me, mam.'

'Oh aye, an since when as Char bin inta football!'

He produces a plastic football from the carrier (had to be the cheapest thing in the whole catalogue) and hands it to me. I'd have loved that car.

'Ta Colin.'

He brings out a slim box like a magician with rabbits and gives it to mam. In it, is a gold necklace which must've cost a bomb!

'Abandon them bangers, love. Le's go fera chinky or summin.'

He catches her round the waist and they have a really long snog. How obscene! In front of me and Char. Where did he get the money from? Mam echoed my thoughts.

'Col? 'ow d' yew buy this lot, eh?'

'Don' say thanks then!'

She pecked him, but carried on.

'I ope it's legal?'

'Jest come up on-a orses, tha's all.'

I hit low and hard.

'Colin? Yew wouldn' do summin like tha Rudge's job, would yew?'

I can't flatten his mood though.

'Don' be darft, Winston ... the silly buggers what done that didn take nothin!'

He's got me against the ropes. I leave the ball on the kitchen floor and ignore Char's pleas for help with her new car. I watch the Welsh news and there's a bit on Rudge's. In view of the deliberate sabotage, they say, the Council have dropped plans to take the company to court. I'm totally bewildered.

After school next day, I meet Leggo outside the Post Office shooting his mouth off about the two men in the Beetle, how he'd told his dad and they were going to the police. I tell him to shut it if he knows what's good for him, but he keeps on about English outsiders coming in and taking over.

'Oh aye, so what's yewr mam then?'

'She's different. She lives yer.'

'Well, most people in Blaen f—in ate Rudge's an yew know it!'

'Not the ones oo bloody work 'ere don'.'

I leave him to think he's won. He's so biased and does-n't even live that near the tip.

The mystery of the break-in had nagged all day. I was hunting the final clue.

Once I get home I pick up the local rag, the *Cwmtaff Express* (or 'Depress', as most say). Colin's watching Scoobydoo on telly and Char's ramming my feet with her car.

The front page headlines are 'ECO TERROR HITS BLAENMORLAIS!!!' with three exclamations. I read it slowly, whispering longer words to myself. The manager is appalled. Police blame outsiders, they'd had reports it seemed (that's probably Leggo and his old man). The Council could not support any campaign against the company. Terror tactics had been used. No hard evidence had been found however.

No evidence? Right by the gap there must've been material from a combat jacket. It was clearer what had happened, who the men were and who paid Colin. He rubs his socks together and looks so smug. I vow to confront him at the right moment, with mam as a witness, hoping for the knockout. I also vow to leave my dreams be in future. They'd have to sort themselves out.

Grudgebands

To be honest, I can't wait to get out. Not from school, you understand – Pencwm is fine as it goes – but from this dump of a town. Cwmtaff is the sweaty armpit of the universe. If God created the world in 7 days, then he left the last millisecond for my place of birth. I always wanted to ask those fundamentalist preachers who visit our school how their Lord could create somewhere as scummy as this.

Planting a load of flowers in the precinct won't improve matters either. The cinema collapsed on the same day its owner had a heart-attack and all it is now is a painted sign saying 'CASTLE FLICKS' fronting a door of solid brick. We haven't even got a swimming-pool, unless you count Morlais Baths, a converted puddle. What is there, but to get ratted for the rest of your life to get away from the boredom, till even that gets boring? No, I'm determined to make it out and away, which is where the school comes in.

It's a new year and a new opportunity. This year I shall choose subjects to suit me, but English is central to my ambitions. I dream of being a sports journalist: TV, radio, papers, I don't care which. If Jimmy Hill can be paid to come out with half-soaked remarks, there's hope yet.

(And it's Neil James interviewing Ryan Giggs before the World Cup Final in Paris, Wales v. Brazil....

'Ryan, you're actually playing for your country instead of Man. Utd. How come? Has it got something to do with the importance of this match?'

'Er ... um ....')

But who do I have for English this year? The one and only 'Terror' Thomson, that's who. I'd come across him several times in the corridors, a mild-mannered charming man. My dad told me he used to play rugby with him and he was a lovely fella off the field.

'What about on it, dad?'

'Ah well, that might explain is nickname. On the other and, I can't remember im being called it then.'

Clear as ditchwater, my dad. But my mam said one of her school friends went out with him and he was 'a real gentleman'. 'Too much so,' she added, leaving me totally intrigued.

I had heard tales to justify the 'Terror': chasing a pupil out of his room with a chair-leg and, even worse, kicking a boy called Ratty in the goolies as he lay on the floor. It was hard to connect these with the blazered, faintly-smiling man who confronted us with the first comprehension 'to really test us'.

English had been fascinating last year. I had 'Doc' Stewart, a true eccentric with trousers torn at the knees and Doc Marten boots banned to us. His posh English accent could've been why he got away with it. He was heavily into reggae and made us talk about our dreams. He'd painted a huge mural of Dylan Thomas covering one of his walls, with a giant fag which looked like a spliff from his mouth. I loved his lessons. He played the rock music we liked as background to written work. His worst threat was 'Carry on talking and I'll turn it to Classic FM!'

Now Mr Thomson was handing out these sheets which resembled exams and we were all suffering from culture shock. We were disappointed and wary.

One thing interested us about Thomson and it wasn't his voice. He droned on and on about the techniques of answering questions. Everyone was getting restless. Whenever Thomson turned to jot a point on the board, Kerry Richards would blow his sheet to make it jump on his desk. I'd briefed Chrissy Evans to ask about our one fascination when the time was right and finally he raised a hand as if stretching from a yawn, which is probably what Thomson thought he was doing as he ignored him at first. Eventually 'Terror' got the message, as Chrissy waved desperately.

'Yes, you boy ... with the haircut!'

We guffawed at Chrissy's 'permsprungtechnik' and then shared his embarrassment. A fine line in sarcasm, but hardly terrorist tactics.

'Mr Ter ... Thomson. Did yew ewsed t' teach The Flood?'

'The Flood? .... I take it you mean the pop group, The Big Flood?'

Chrissy nodded eagerly and beamed. Most of us now gave our full attention, even Matthew 'the Martian' Bates, who must've known that early Flood songs were sci-fi epics.

'Yes I did ... now let's get back to the comprehension.'

'Terror' Thomson refused to be human. He'd just thrown away his one chance of real contact with our class. I knew he'd regret it, but he didn't. He thought he was doing the right thing, keeping a distance.

From that moment, little things were done to test him out. He thought he was testing us, but it was the other way round.

Amazingly, he didn't live up to his nickname, though I could see his temperature rising when Jason Leigh said

61

someone had nicked his pen and Melanie Davies pogoed in front of him to go to the 'bogs', as she put it. I could see he was trying to contain something by the way he kept jangling keys in his trouser pocket.

The work was basic enough and I coped well with it. He came round and praised me, which I didn't like. When he informed me (loud enough for the class to hear) that he used to play 'rugger' with my dad, I felt like tearing up my paper and binning it on the way out.

Afterwards, I thought I'd get it from Kerry, but he knew that I'd give as much back, so he didn't pursue the matter. Kerry fancied himself as a footballer, but made Vinnie Jones seem like a ball-juggler. Whereas, I've played for the county and could show him up any day.

By an extraordinary coincidence, a new year at Pencwm also meant a new club, started by Mr Bob 'the dog' Jones, who used to be a guitarist in loads of local bands. At first I turned up – like many there – with the main motive being to get out of the September rain. What's more, there was no sport Friday lunchtime, because the Games teachers went up the pub.

Bob's nickname is a mystery to me, but Siân Jones assured me it had something to do 'with bonkin positions'. How she knows I haven't the foggiest! Anyway, the pop or rock club was divided between heavy metal hairies, those into the charts and the anti-rain brigade, some of whom were into bands from the past like The Flood, who were now trendy because their lyrics sounded as if they'd been on magies. There was a big debate about the club's name and I practically dozed off near the radiator. My ears pricked when a magazine was mentioned by Mr Jones. Before I knew it, I was editor of the journal, to be called *Grudge* (as opposed to grunge). It was a compromise between heavies and poppers and was preferred to the imaginative *Pop the Dog* or practical *In the Dry* (which had nothing to do with music!).

I volunteered an exclusive interview with Mr Thomson and Bob 'the dog' promised he'd try to set it up, though he didn't sound too optimistic.

I think my dad's rugby connection must've done it, because Mr Jones organized it for the following Friday in Thomson's room. I began racking my brain for relevant questions: 'What was Kid Barnett's favourite subject at school?' 'Did Kevin Pearce ever get the cane?' For a while, the obvious didn't occur to me. Then I thought of Pearce's most famous song, 'School Prison', about a teacher who attacked pupils. The chorus went:

You're a jailer
You're a hangman
Keeping kids in prison
Hey teacher, open up the doors!

It was so catchy, it made everyone sing along and Ben Summers' lead guitar lifted the roof off like a mass breakout, inmates running for the hills.

The question was obvious, but how to phrase it? 'Does the character in 'School Prison' resemble anybody from Pearce's old school?' It sounded reasonable, but I couldn't imagine Thomson being forthcoming. Still, my journalistic career had to start somewhere and – in the absence of sports writing – the one thing I did know about was The Flood.

English was as dire as Cwmtaff and Thomson began to live up to his nickname, throwing minor wobblies. He tried to be tough and boasted about his days playing for top class rugby teams in England, but the more macho he became, the more we sensed his weakness. It was like a sport and I could've commentated:

And it's 'Terror' Thomson in the black corner coming in with the first uppercut, a blow of 'Yes, you will need a pen, even though you can hardly write.' 9B in the blue corner (school uniform colour) hit back with a succession of vicious punches to the head like... 'This is mega borin!', 'Why carn we read a play?' and 'The bloke oo wrote is musta bin trippin!' to send Thomson reeling to the floor and almost out for the count. He only just manages to stagger to his feet and is... saved by the bell again.

Worse than English was the fact that Melanie Davies was after me. I used to sit on the back of the bus up to Pwll where we both live, she in Gwaun Terrace and myself in posher Brecon Villas. I used to sit with the boys and have a good laugh till she decided to plonk herself there and blow smoke into my face, a sure sign of affection.

I attempted talking to my dad before he went down the golf club.

'English is a bummer, dad.'

'What's wrong with ol Terror Thomson? He's been alright, hasn't he?'

'Nothin's workin out ... an tha bloody Melanie Davies is arfta me.'

'Steer clear of her, Neil. You don't want to catch any dubious diseases.'

He wouldn't take anything seriously and I couldn't discuss it with my mam or she'd get too upset and get me some private tutor in English before I knew it.

Anyway, *Grudge* and my interview were something else and I focussed on them, ignoring the rest as far as I could. In his room and out of lesson time, Thomson was relaxed and proved a mine of information. He drank tea and spoke into my tape-machine so warmly I forgot he was a teacher. We were budding reporter and intervie-wee. He told me he'd only taught two of The Flood in Oxford, but they were the two main song-writers of the early days. Kid Barnett had been a scout and Kevin Pearce a very promising basketball player. It was a long way from the band's image of psychedelic weirdoes, most likely inspired by acid. Especially Barnett. It was impos-sible to imagine the author of the legendary 'Sun Fish Dream' around a campfire singing about riding along on the crest of a wave.

I kept the crunch question till last and I could see that Thomson was disturbed by it. His hand crept into his pocket to jiggle keys. He paused, then spoke very delib-erately.

'To be honest, I never liked Pearce. Always thought he had a grudge – the name of your magazine, I believe – he could've based that song on a few teachers. It might even have been me.... I found him extremely arrogant.'

This fitted with the history of The Big Flood, though Thomson didn't know it. After four albums, Pearce had split from the band, gone solo and scorned the rest of the group, calling them talentless. Ironically, the others had kept the group's name and been far more successful than him.

After the interview, I told him what had happened to Kid Barnett. How drugs had addled his brain-cells and he'd suffered several nervous breakdowns. He said how sorry he was and that Barnett had been 'a nice lad'. He stared at me fixedly.

'You know, Neil. You remind me of him. Ambitious

but friendly. Don't get dragged down, will you? And please change the name of your magazine.'

'I'll see what I cun do, sir. Thanks very much f' doin the interview.'

'A pleasure.'

The next week elastic bands took over and any boy without some was either a swot or a wimp. It was the delayed initiation ceremony for new or supply teachers, or those we hated. I risked a flick at Kerry in History when we had a supply, but that didn't really count, except for Melanie who was so impressed she offered me a fag on the way home.

'No, ta. I'm in trainin.'

'So am I, but I won' tell yew wha for!'

Shakespeare was responsible for the worst upsurge in rubber warfare. Mr Thomson introduced us to him with the immortal words 'You won't like it, but you've got to do it if you want to pass English.'

The girls could always hazard more awkward questions and Siân Jones kept repeating 'Why?' to everything 'Terror' lectured us on. She was like a persistent infant. In the end, he promised a film later in the week. Chrissy got all excited wanting to know if 'Arnie Schwartnigger' was in it (that's the way he pronounced it). Faces dropped when Thomson explained it would be a cartoon version of Shakespeare, to help us understand the play.

A blacked-up room and the possibility of a comedy – which 'Terror' said wasn't supposed to be funny – meant that almost every boy stocked up fur 'A Midsummer Night's Battle'. As soon as the lights went out and the screen showed lovers, fairies and a bloke called Bottom Weaver talking gobbledeegook, strange elastic insects were propelled through the air. Melanie sat by me and I felt her tights against my left thigh. I manoeuvred away to avoid a rapid reaction force.

Just as this fairy servant called Puck was flying around and 'Terror' warned us that we'd return to his room if there was 'any more silliness', I was struck on the cheek by a band which stung like a hornet.

'F—in ell. Oo done that?' I blurted, not thinking.

'Terror' swivelled round, glared and moved at an incredible rate. He snapped on the lights, pushed the video to off and scooped up the missile near me. His face was close to mine and he spat and sweated as he yelled.

'Don't dare use such language in my class, Neil James! I'm astonished at you! ... And who did do that? I want to know! NOW!'

I was covered with his gob. I had no idea who was responsible, but knew at that point why he was called 'Terror'. It was there in his eyes. He was terrified. Terrified of losing, of failing, of not being able to cope.

He must've noticed my recognition, because he backed off. He was equally furious with the class as a whole.

'You'll all stay in at breaktime until I find out which one of you pathetic, childish little morons did this!'

He held the elastic band up like a limp condom. I wiped my face in my jumper sleeve as vague protests were mumbled.

'And Neil James! I thought you had more sense!'

He thought he'd picked an easy target. He was wrong.

'It's Shakespeare, sir.'

'What do you mean? Shakespeare flicked the band, did he?'

'It drives everyone mad. There's no point to it!'

'Well, you'd better make a choice and quick. Because you're going to need it. It's as simple as that!'

I didn't reply. He thought he'd won. Nobody owned up and he switched the video back on. He stood at the front, scanning us, ready to pounce. He pretended to forget about keeping us in. I could see his relief when the bell went. He called me over.

'Your father would be ashamed of you, Neil.'

He was trying to be chummy, to make up for spitting too much.

'I never done nothin anyway.'

'That's not the attitude. Don't turn out like Kevin Pearce. Off you go and let's not see that kind of outburst again.'

Curiously I thought he was addressing himself more than me. On the bus, Melanie was ecstatic, telling everyone how I'd mouthed off at 'Terror' and called Shakespeare rotten.

When I got home, the first thing I did was put on 'School Prison', with maximum volume so Melanie could hear it in Gwaun Terrace. I sang along to the chorus with Pearce and shared his feeling. I played it again and this time my mam shouted, 'Neil! Turn it down, love! My ead's splittin!'

I didn't give a toss. My feet thumped the floorboards. If I had my way, *Grudge* it would remain.

Botched Experiment

Am I in heaven? White walls, though they're smudgy. Can't be. I remember what I've done. Some in-between place maybe?

What did they call it in Church? Purgatory? Through the slits of my vision I can see my mam and younger brothers. Are they here to say goodbye to me? My mam's gazing beyond, out of the window presumably. I can hear their voices rushing through me like the noise of cars on the road outside my bedroom. My head's a smog of cloud and exhaust fumes.

Suffocated from the inside.

Did I do the right thing? If she is saying a last good-bye, why isn't she holding my hand? Why is Shane withdrawn into his hooded jacket, scoffing a bar of chocolate? Why is the baby (I call him that, though he's a toddler) pushing a chair and squealing?

My stomach's a raw wound refusing to heal. Every pump from my heart releases a flow of pain. Pain which at least makes me seem alive. A living death?

I close my eyes on purpose in case she notices. If this is really a waiting-place who will judge? An unmarked grave outside the church walls beckons. I want to hurt them all. I want them to know what they have done. I want to be buried along with that secret worry which nags every second.

The sounds disappear. The traffic halts. Even the fumes go away, though they lurk somewhere there in the upper skies.

I am being baptised. An angel in white is washing me. The walls have changed to a shiny blue material.

'Am I there yet?'

She's black. She smiles and I want to stay here forever, to be looked after by her.

'It depends where you want to be,' she goes about her business as if she'd never saved me.

Her hands shift me around like a sack of spuds. Also, I feel like a baby again when I see her ample breasts as she bends, their warmth close by.

'You're a silly boy!' she says, as she props me up.

'Why?'

'You know. You shouldn't waste your life.'

I don't want to see anything else, but she pulls back the blue and reveals a hospital ward. She has a mark on her forehead. She's Indian (I saw a telly programme on it). I know boys from the school who'd call her a 'Paki'. Not that school means much to me: nobody tends you there, you're on your own.

She busies away to the next bed and leaves me. I've failed. To keep someone you have to create a big scene and even then it didn't do my dad any good, wandering the streets like a complete 'eejit' (as mam would say), burbling on about being the new Messiah.

What shall I do? Fall out of bed? Scream in hysterical agony? I close my eyes again instead and think of the possibilities. What's left? My bedroom at home isn't even safe! I went upstairs and found some friend of my eldest brother Marc burrowing into one of my drawers.

'Ey, wha's goin on?'

'Oh! Sorry! Thought it woz Marc's room.'

People coming and going through the house like a station platform. Not a place to hide my thoughts in. And my mam never there, especially when she sat with the telly on, bottles lined and empty as her expression, her fag-smoke I suck in to stain save on buying. I feel her presence more when she's away on one of her trips with her fancy man, cos then I want her around, I actually miss her. When she's there I know what she thinks: six kids, six burdens. She was too old too young. I might just help with her financial problems.

All I wanted was trainers. No flashing light jobs, or pump action. Just tidy enough so the kids round here wouldn't take the piss all the time. Mine are so small my toes see daylight, so holey they could stand for Pope.

'I'll get you some, sure I will Liam. Soon as I've paid off the electric.'

Yes, and the gas and the water and ... it was lies! Always lies! That's why I'd climbed the lamppost outside our house. That's why I'd refused to come down till I had those trainers. Other kids got them: their parents stole or did work on the side to pay for them.

Marc had tried to persuade me down, 'I'll get some, Liam. C'mon down, yew'll end up in a loony bin! I know a bloke cun get some dead cheap.'

He probably did, but it wasn't the same. It wasn't like trying them on in a Sports Shop, admiring myself, walking round. Mam by me, taking notice for once.

In the end, cold, hunger and my own resolve to do one better made up my mind.

There's a bustling, roaring noise so I think my family have returned. The ward fills with visitors and approaching me is this girl in school uniform.

''Elen! What yew doin yer?'

She draws a chair to my bedside, goes a bit pink and twiddles with her permed hair.

'Come t' see yew, dafto .... I yeard.'

'Ow?'

'Seen Marc down town.'

'Oh aye.'

'Yew look ... sorta white. I carn get over it.'

'Thanks a lot!'

She laughs nervously, 'No, I mean ... yew look fine, onest. It's jes that I aven seen yew fer ages. Las time yew were in school wuz when yew woz in that ome.'

'Safe ouse, they called it.'

'Why don' yew come t' school no more?'

'Bin sent yer by a bunkie or wha?'

'No way. I jest wanted t' see yew. ... Like, we ewsed t' talk so long before. Carn I elp?'

She doesn't want to ask, not directly and I don't want to answer either. It had been a cock-up after all. Helen's attractive, no doubt about it. She's plumpish, not fat and thinks her figure's all wrong. Her eyes say everything: full of energy, eagerness, sharing. I don't want to bury her with me.

'Na! S'orright. onest!'

Her right hand tugs at the bedclothes now repeatedly. She wants to catch hold of me, but daren't. I wish I could think of something she could do. It's as though that man has put a curse upon me. It's as if he's given me some disease and if I find myself looking at another boy....

We talk about my family and how nothing has changed.

I tell her to forget my problems, but she says she never will. After our so longs, I grip the quilt where her hand was, remember her smile and vow to take it with me wherever it is I'm going.

I drift back to my last time at school. The people at

Ty Derwyn insisted I went, encouraging me, not like my mam who only cared when there was a chance of a fine. Things went okay and my uniform was neat and clean, not like at home.

Some teachers were really sarky, saying stuff like, 'Well Liam, I must say you've grown since the last time I saw you.'

Sparky Rees welcomed me, obviously believing my time lazing around had been spent in a detention centre or drug-dealing on the streets. I played along by saying as little as possible, to get him thinking.

'Ey! They all ewse yewer ouse Liam. I know coz I seen em.'

'Yew're right, Sparky mun. But I don' know nothin, see!'

'Oh aye. Naturally!'

When I returned home – cos it could only be temporary – there was no purpose left in me. The whole atmosphere took over: Marc's rave music pounding all day long, his friends skinning up and the booze I swigged when I was down, which was more often. The drink became my best friend. It blanked me out into the night. Without it I couldn't sleep. I stopped dreaming though. My sleep became the walls of a prison, no colour and no mirror.

Deva, the lush nurse whose face brought me back to life, tells me that today my mam's coming to take me home. Out there in Cwmtaff, my dad's ready to jump out of an alley and throw water over me, blessing and forgiving me for being possessed by 'that demon whore!' Out there in Cwmtaff, is that man walking free before the court-case, whose grin follows me like the Cheshire cat from 'Alice'

– I loved that when I was little. A grin I can't swipe off except with the anaesthetic of alcohol. That man my mam trusted cos he knew her boyfriend. Who took me away to give her a fraction more space, one less worry for a while. It'll be one down, five to go. I'll approach this botched experiment of my life in a scientific way. Next time, I'll get it right.

A Prayer for Liam

After visiting Liam Connell in hospital I hoped he'd come back to school, but he never did. I could talk to him more openly than any other boy. He liked me and other girls, but I never sensed I was other than a friend, someone to load his feelings onto. I accepted them willingly. He needed me as a person, not like Jason Leigh who I'd gone with once and who couldn't wait to let his hands 'go walkies' at the disco. Afterwards, I told him where to go – a very hot place he'd end up anyway – and he and his willing mates started calling me 'frigit' in lessons. Typical! They couldn't even pronounce it properly.

Then the terrible news came, in Assembly of all places. We knew something was up because one of the Deputy Heads, Mr Richards arrived near the end to take over from our Head of Year, Mrs Watkins. Mrs Watkins had spent the Assembly trying to be kind, not giving off as usual, so we were prepared. Old Richards is a sturdy man, but he seemed to shrink behind the lectern as he addressed us.

'I have something really sad to tell you, Year 9. It concerns a boy who – though he hasn't been in school often – has had awful problems to overcome.'

Me and my friend Cathy shared knowing looks. I wanted to rush out straight away, afraid I'd break down.

'I'm very sorry to say that Liam Connell died early this morning.'

In the silence of everyone, I could hear myself sighing and swallowing for breath. Most of them hardly knew him. How could they understand? I stared angrily at the ground. I was so relieved when Richards whispered, 'Let us pray'. He spoke of Liam, a boy who'd tried hard, but it wasn't about him. I fixed my eyelids together to stop tears from burning. Cathy put her arm round me. She was like that, didn't care if we'd be called 'Lezzies'. She had a mouth on her like garden shears. I didn't take in the rest of the prayer or the others leaving. I sat thinking of Liam in hospital, wishing I'd left him with a solution. I could've done much more. Could I have asked my parents to take him in? No, that was absurd. I was still guilty, I hadn't made an effort.

'C'mon, Hel,' Cathy kept repeating. She went quiet. The first time I'd known her short of words.

Close now, Mrs Watkins sounded unfamiliar and caring.

''elen, love, I know it's a terrible loss. We all liked im.'

Though she was tender and put her hand on my shoulder, I felt bitter. They'd given up because he was beyond help. He wouldn't come to school, so he was a lost statistic. When he did go, nobody was concerned enough to listen.

'I know what appened!' I confronted her, shaking off her hand and Cathy's arm simultaneously.

'What d' yew mean?' she jerked back because of my harshness, her voice losing its softness.

'Ee didn jes die, did ee? Ee killed imself. I'm right, in I?'

'I don' think he meant to.... It was a cry for attention.'

She produced that well-worn phrase because she had no idea. How could she? Cathy was talking, on her feet defending me. She'd make a great lawyer one day.

'Miss! Jes leave er alone, please. She went t' see Liam

in ospital, see. Ee talked to er more 'an anyone.'

'Okay. Why don' yew girls go to the nurse's room? Join in lessons when yew feel able to. If yew want to discuss things, yew know where t' find me.'

She was her brusque, practical self again. Me and Cathy would've been happy to stay in the Hall, but to please her we went to the nurse's. On the way I told Cathy how I felt responsible.

''el, no way! Yew jes carn feel like tha. What the ell could yew ave done?'

'I dunno ... maybe gone out with im?'

'I don think ee liked any girls tha way.'

'Ow d' yew mean?'

'Well, I int sayin ee wuz gay.'

'What the bloody ell does it matter now, Cathy?'

'Okay, okay.'

We reached the nurse's and she was tending a Year 7er with a nosebleed. She asked us for notes. Cathy drew her aside as if she was a member of Staff and whispered to her.

The nurse said we could stay in her 'quiet room'. I lay on the couch and it reminded me of telly sketches about shrinks. Cathy by my side like the psychiatrist.

She began to jabber, when I needed a chance to think. My insensitive comment about how pale he'd looked kept cutting away with the sharp snipping of Cathy's advice: ''el, what yew need is someone or summin. Yew carn jest brood on Liam an wha's appened. Yew're too bound up with school work. Yew should come out more with-a girls.'

'Wha? Street corners an bus-shelters yew mean?'

'Oh, c'mon 'el, we do go down town.'

'Listen, Cathy. I know yew're tryin t' elp, but there's

on'y one thin I wanna think about right now, s' do me a favour an save yewer breath!'

I was surprised at how cruel I sounded and, as Cathy got up to leave I called her back.

'Cathy mun, I didn mean it like tha. I jes mean nothin else matters now. Ev'rythin else seems so ... small.'

Then she came out with something really important, not DIY patching of emotions.

'Write it down!'

'Eh?'

'Write it in poetree or summin. Yew know wha Doc Stewart always tol us? If yew feel summin strong enough, then stick it down on paper.'

'Aye, I jest might.'

She'd planted a seed. I knew I could water and nurture it. I could speak to Liam now he was in heaven. I hoped he'd listen to my prayer. I was sure he was there. He'd been in trouble, but done nothing seriously wrong. All his problems were piled on by his family situation.

I never returned to lessons that day. Cathy persuaded Mrs Watkins to let me go early. My mam drove up during her lunch-hour to take me home. In our car I cried and cried, eyes puffing up and stinging.

'Tha's right, 'clen love, yew ave a good cry. I didn know yew liked im that much mind ... they're a crazy famlee.'

I didn't respond. All the feelings I'd spent the morning keeping down quaked my body. It was like when my dad used to shake me for being naughty when I was small. No punishing hands, only mine clutching my trousers to stop their shaking.

My mam insisted on staying with me, ringing work to explain. She gave me no practical tips, but cups of tea. She asked loads of questions, anxious to find what she was convinced I was keeping secret.

'Did yew go out with im a lot, love?'

She tried to appear casual, but in her own way was interrogating. She thought I was covering up.

'I never did at all. We woz jest friendly.'

'Whatever yew say, love. But why didn yew tell me yew wen' up Prince Charles?'

'Oh, im as well now, is it?' I laughed the last of the tears away.

'Don' be s' silly, 'elen!'

She got the message and went to the kitchen. I sneaked upstairs, hoping she'd leave me be.

Warily, I peered in the mirror. Tears had swelled my face, so I looked even fatter. Liam had always reassured me by saying 'pleasantly plump' (for a boy who could hardly write, he had a way with words), but it made no difference. My dad was podgy and I took after him. My perm was knotty. A complete mess! It was all very well Cathy saying get somebody, but who was going to fancy an overweight bush baby? Only Liam maybe and now, where was he?

I rummaged for a biro under the junkheap on my desktop. My mam hadn't tidied it, I think she'd given up. I found one eventually and also a pad of A4. I didn't know what my prayer was going to be like. As I lifted my pen, my mam called out: ''elen! Are yew orright?'

If she'd been closer, I'd have been tempted to stab her eyeballs with it. I put on my best, sweetest voice.

'Yeh, mam ... thanks ... jest avin a rest.'

'Okay! Let me know if yew need anythin!'

'Yeh, inspiration,' I spoke, then shouted down, 'I will mam!'

I needed a first line, or even a heading. I played with

my hair so it got into a knot. Finally, I wrote:

Liam, I need you
To talk to again
I listened to you
You listened to me
We were like twins.
I'm praying now
That you're in heaven.
I've cried once too often....

I couldn't think of any more. It definitely wasn't finished. I'd written poems for Doc last year, about my dreams, about my worst phobias. I really meant it this time.

My only way of communication.

I fiddled with my perm again, as I must've done that time at Liam's bedside. Lunchtime in school, standing by the mobiles, I'd discovered him on his own. Cathy was at drama practice and I was wandering aimlessly. He was smoking.

'Hiya Liam!'

'Hiya El! Wanna fag?'

'No ta, don' smoke. I should though, jest t' lose weight.'

'Ow d' fags make yew lose weight 'en?'

'Yew eat em instead o' food, silly!'

For a street-wise kid, he could be so naive.

'Oh, I adn thought o' tha. Anyway, yew don' need t' lose weight. Yew look fine t' me.'

Most other boys would've been lying to get something. Not Liam. He was honest as an infant and I smiled as if he'd given me a present. He was pale and skinny: my opposite.

'Wish I woz yewer build.'

'Don' be darft, there's no tits on me!'

We giggled and couldn't stop, ticklish laughter which became hysterical when he spluttered on his fag and almost swallowed it. His face was creased like I'd never seen it.

When we came round, we opened up. I told him how lonely and pampered I felt as an only child, then felt ashamed as he recounted his woes. I couldn't imagine how one boy could have so many difficulties and still be standing there joking. He stood firm against the mobiles wall, yet dragged incessantly.

I wrote again.

Both alone you and me
Opposites yet the same
If you're looking down
I hope you'll forgive
My insensitivity.
Send me a reply
Give me a sign
So I know. . . .

'So I know' – what? The ending stumped me. I could leave it open, but there were too many doubts. If Liam were to hear, he'd think I hadn't bothered.

I pulled at my cheeks to feel the flab there. I'd go on a diet of fags in honour of his memory, munching away down to the stubs.

'I wanna get away y' know, El. An I don' mean jes run away from ome neither.'

'But yewr mam? I'm shewer she cares. Deep down I bet she does.'

'She's gotta funny way o' showin it 'en ... na! She don' wan' none of us. She ates us. We've taken er freedom.'

So I know you've got your freedom.

That was it! It worked. I read through the poem and it flowed. Previously they'd been a toil. This came from another place within me, I'm not sure where exactly.

Where was he most likely to hear it? By the mobiles, our spot? By his grave eventually? Or even at the lamp-post in his street he'd climbed that time? I decided all these were right and a church would be as well, because he was still a Catholic, though his mam had removed him from St. Kevin's.

Nobody else must hear me, nobody know. This would be tricky near the mobiles.

''elen! Tea's ready! 'urry up an come down!'

My mam's commands dragged me to earth. My poem and its recitation would have to remain in my drawer for another time.

I woke up next day with a real sense of purpose. I was disappointed to find it sunny, but didn't think it would last, as October in Cwmtaff usually promised a rainy season lasting till the summer drought!

I heard the paper jammed into our letter-box and my parents whispering. At breakfast my dad was very supportive, but I couldn't help feeling that they both wanted to say, 'Don't mix with someone like him again!' Because they'd bought our council house they thought they were superior. Trainee snobs I'd call them, though I knew they wanted what was best for me.

When I used teletext to get the local weather, my mam

was convinced I'd gone mad. Normally, I wouldn't come round till lunchtime. Showery tomorrow: I was delighted!

'The funeral won' be s' soon, if yew're thinkin bout-a weather for that, 'el.'

'I know tha mam ... it's jest ... I think I got Games today an I wanna know if I should pack my ockey kit.'

They were both glad, assuming I'd got over it easily. My dad gave me a warmlips kiss as he rushed off to work.

'Where's-a paper mam?' I asked as she cleared the table.

'It's late. Don' think it come ... 'less yewr dad took it t' work.'

'Thought I yeard it delivered?'

'No, I don' think so. ... Now, urry up f' school, or yew'll be late!'

It made no difference. I walked through the Shops and bought a *Western Mail* on the way. I stood in an alley where kids wouldn't go and read it. Front page, main story: an old photo of Liam when he was about nine. He wore a scruffy tee-shirt and was trying to grin, but managed to look silly. The headlines were SOCIAL SERVICES BLAMED FOR SCHOOLBOY'S SUICIDE. The report said how his elder brother had found him hanging. He'd used his school tie. I didn't even know Liam had one! Mrs Connell blamed Social Services because they'd failed to counsel him before a court-case due next month. She explained that the accused only lived two streets away and Liam had seen him around. His name couldn't be disclosed for legal reasons.

Mrs Connell had shifted the blame. Liam had never told me about the case. What had that man done to him? I wanted to feel angry, but was full of sadness and pity.

I was too heavy. I was bloated with it. My legs filled those pipe-like, black trousers.

'She's off all-a time with er fancy man. Richie she calls im. I'd call im Dick!'

Liam by the mobiles returned to me. I went back in the Spar and asked for a packet of Regal for my dad. They knew me there as a polite girl and should trust me.

'For your father, are you sure?'

'Yeh, onest.'

'Okay then.'

I put them in the bottom of my bag and ran to school. I was late for registration and lied that I hadn't slept much last night, because of all the upset. It worked due to my harrassed expression. Cathy eyed me curiously.

The day had little meaning. I went to the mobiles breaktime, but a group of boys stood in Liam's place. Tomorrow and the rain, I kept thinking.

Cathy asked me at lunch if I'd read the paper or seen the local news on telly. She'd been holding it in all morning. I didn't feel like going into it and when she pursued details as if it were a soap opera, I snapped.

'Cathy mun! Leave it be, will yew? The papers blow ev'rythin up. Yew know tha.'

She'd had enough of me as well, and avoided me the rest of the day.

At home that evening I found my room neat and clean. In my top desk-drawer the poem was where I'd left it, but I had this sense that mam had been through everything. Probably searching for femidoms or photos of Liam semi-naked. It annoyed me that she might have read it and also her lies about the paper. I snatched the poem and scribbled the title: 'A Prayer for Liam'. I folded and placed it in my jeans pocket, stomping downstairs, making a performance of each step.

My dad wasn't home yet and mam was laying the table. I crashed the living-room door open.

'Wha's the matter?'

'Mam! ave yew bin through my stuff?'

'I wuz tidyin up! Yew wouldn even bother....'

'Listen mam! I know fera fact the paper come this mornin! An please leave my private things alone, will yew?'

'Don' shout at me like that, young lady!'

'Yew won' find anythin anyway!'

Out the front door, slamming it ferociously so the neighbours took notice and could complain (to mam's horror): 'Well, 'ey mighta bought theyr ouse, but 'ey're jest as bard as evr'yone!' My mam wouldn't follow, afraid to draw attention.

I sped up the hill. It was too light really, but clouds were gathering with my anticipation. I hadn't planned this, but now was the opportunity. I knew roughly where the Connells lived, not far from school at the top of the estate.

All the Closes and Roads ridiculously named after flowers. 'Daffodil Alley, where I belong' ... one of mam's Rod Stewarts came to me, transformed. Sunflower Close, Dahlia Avenue. Why not vegetables? Leek Street sounded alright.

I passed the Greens, an area of grass near the Community Centre. Gary Crissle was playing football with his younger brother. He waved and shouted out. Someone else – in a Man. Utd kit – waved too. It was Tracey Estebanez who was a tomboy, but a great footballer everyone said. All I knew about soccer was my

Ryan Giggs posters and I suppose I liked him because the others did.

I waved back and made for Poppy Road. Somehow I knew I'd locate the house and I was right. One down-stairs window was boarded up. The front door was split and the garden was worse than my room before mam attacked it with a hoover. Black rubbish bags and rusty bikes littered the lawn. I expected to see used condoms in the flower-beds, except they were Catholics!

The lamppost was further up the road. I'd forgotten the fags so that part of the ritual must wait. I passed the lamppost and stopped, gazing up at the school fence, its lines of grey spears. I took out my poem and unfolded it. How not to stand out? Not everybody recited poems to lampposts on Penôl Estate! At least, not till the pubs had shut!

What the hell! I stood, my back to the house, hugging-distance from it, holding the poem against it. I hoped no strays would come this way and cock a leg! I began to read out my prayer to Liam, trying to concentrate on his spirit there, where he'd escaped. Was this an aerial, a mast to transmit? I made each syllable clear as I could, till a woman's yell interrupted.

'If you're the press youse'll ave t' wait till I get dressed!'

I turned. Liam's mam was leaning out of a top win-dow, barely concealed by a flimsy nightgown. Her eyes were deep in their sockets and her grey-flecked hair straggly, yet I could tell she'd once been pretty. She must've noticed how young I was: even without uniform, no way did I resemble a newshound.

'Who are y' an what d' y' want?'

Before I'd time to answer, a taxi came round the corner and spilled out its contents, a tall man who lurched past me, knocking my poem onto the pavement. He never said sorry, but swayed on the path, sending missiles of abuse up at Mrs Connell.

'Yew better come down yer, y' stupid cow! Ow could yew let im die, my little boy?'

He was obviously drunk and grasped hold of the lamp-post for support.

I picked up my poem and scurried away, hearing the man scream out 'I'll smash the whool f—in lot of them, 'less yew come an talk t' me!'

I moved faster than I ever did playing hockey. I thought the police would soon arrive and didn't want to be around.

The drunk must've been Liam's dad, though he didn't sound Irish.

When I reached home I went to my room avoiding my parents completely. My dad came up and asked me to apologize to my mam, which I thought was a cheek. I was so stubborn, he gave up. Half a poem was better than none and maybe Liam's spirit would be intrigued, wondering what was to come.

I couldn't believe the sun the next day. I'd been cheated by Bert Fish. I would write and complain. However, in the distance were ominous clouds which gave me hope.

At breakfast, mam tried to make it up, while dad kept tactfully quiet.

'Listen, I woz on'y tidyin, love. I couldn elp but see yewr poem ... I shouldn've read it but ... it was lovely, 'el. Yew should read it at-a funeral. I didn know yew woz s' talented.'

She'd won me over, but I was adamant.

'Mam! It's still a private poem. Yew ad no right, see. But don tell no-one else about it ... it's like a prayer, see.'

She was persuaded I shouldn't share my talents.

During tutorial time at school, as drizzle began to fall and turn to heavy rain, I thanked Cathy and she was puzzled.

'Whatever for, 'el?'

'I carn say, but I'll tell yew arfta.'

'Arfta wha? ... Well, yew in arf bin actin weird recently, tha's all I cun say.'

'Nobody's ever died oo's bin close t' me before.'

'Aye ... I'm sorry, 'el.'

'Cathy? Do me a favour, eh?'

'Yeh!'

'Don' come lookin f' me breaktime, right?'

'Orright. ... I ope yewer not gunna do summin darft though?'

'Well ... sort of ... but nothin dangerous.'

When the break-bell rang and everyone headed for halls or to buy cans and crisps, I slipped out of a side-door into the damp. I put on my coat: packet of Regal in one pocket, poem in the other.

By the mobiles, with the paper getting floppy, it was tricky reading as drops teared my eyes. As I read I had a strange sensation. It was as if Liam's spirit was there puffing away in appreciation. I was thrilled and dead scared.

I took out the packet and clumsily fumbled with the wrapping. Liam would've called me a 'smokey virgin'.

'Liam ... if yew're really there ... this is one f' my weight.'

The fag was already limp when I took a bite. I chewed and chewed. Bits stuck in my throat. It was revolting! I swallowed some and felt instantly sick. I coughed and spat some out. I took one more nibble, then threw the box away in disgust. The bits tugged at my stomach like pieces of rope.

I ran back to the side-door, bursting into the building. I had to get to the toilet quick. My face sweating like a fever. I bumped straight into Mr Lloyd, Deputy, a total dragon's breath.

'Why aren't you in your lesson, young lady?'

'I'm sorry ... I ....'

Spewed up at his feet. I tried aiming away from his shining brogues, but spattered them as well as his perfectly-creased striped trousers.

He stepped back, as if he'd had an electric shock. He was speechless for once. When I'd finished retching over the corridor, I leaned against the wall with arms stretched, like a person about to be searched by the drugs squad.

'Get to the nurse and ... I'll talk to you later!' he ordered, back to his normal self.

I think the nurse believed I was using Liam's death to get out of lessons. She even hinted I might be pregnant by him. Wish I'd gone along with her and explained away my fat. I only had about ten minutes before Lloyd came. I could see he was upset about his precious trousers, as he kept looking down at them as he spoke. We went to his office and he said he'd phone my dad unless he got the truth.

'Did you take drugs, Helen? I realise you're not that kind of girl, but....'

He had this way of making you shrink. I was like some Primary kid. He towered over me and he wasn't tall.

'Okay, I'll tell yew the truth....'

'Yes, you'd better had.' He propped himself against his filing-cabinet.

'I swallowed arf a cigarette!'

He squinted, attempting to detect insanity in my still watery eyes.

'Are you being funny with me, my girl?'

'No really, Mr Lloyd. I did. I ate it coz I'm fed up of bein fat. Liam Connell tol me fags woz great f' losin weight so I ate one!'

I put on the little girl lost act and he fell for it. He must've concluded I was a brainy girl with no common-sense.

Either that, or he'd examined my vomit and found strands of tobacco there. I wouldn't put it past him.

'Listen! I know your father you know, Helen. We used to sing in the same choir. If anything like this happens again, I'll make sure he finds out. Understand?'

'It won', sir! Definite!'

'Off you go then, young lady. And take your outside coat off!'

As I walked the depopulated corridors to Welsh, I was content. If I never recited the poem again, I knew his spirit had heard it. I might even let Cathy read it. When I told her about it and the fag she had a fit and howled – 'Don' know about writin a poem f' Liam, I think yew're bloody turnin into im!'

Tracey Kicks

New boots for a new season. My dad and me bought them.

'The way yewr feet keep growin, Trace, yew'd better get a job in a circus, ne' mind football team!'

He went on dreaming for me, but this season was different. I was already too old, see. At thirteen, would you believe? Last season everything seemed to happen: the papers and the telly. And all cos of Southampton showing so much interest. What did I have left? Pennants, a signed ball and a kit which was now too small. I'd been paid off!

Even when we watched *Sgorio* together (my mam complaining cos there was a new series on HTV), I couldn't get excited about dad's commentary. Madrid v. Zaragosa. A Welsh commentary, with English subtitles and my dad doing his best imitation of Alan Parry on a bad day.

'And it's Estebanez jinking down the left wing. She beats three defenders, cuts inside and scores superbly!'

His words didn't match the action either. The ball usually got passed back or sideways, just as I was supposed to be scoring.

'And Real go 1-0 up, after that tremendous goal by Welsh-born Spaniard Tracey Estebanez. Surely Giggs's place in the Welsh team is now under threat?'

'Dad! Both teams are Real and yew know I don' play on-a wing.'

'Wha's up, Trace? Yew look as if yew're about t' do a Gazza.'

My mam thumped the iron down as she did her housework. She was twice as loud when annoyed. My dad supped his can of lager and expected an instant answer.

'It's tha Neil James.'

My mam was glad to join in, thinking we'd shaken off the football talk.

'As ee bin pickin on yew, love?'

'Shut up, will yew mam?'

'There's no need f' tha! Yew cun bloody well go t' bed an switch over-a telly, if yewr goin t' be so ignorant!'

She crashed down the iron as an exclamation mark. But dad didn't co-operate.

'Give er a chance, Joan. Yew don' understand.'

'Well, if yew two 're goin t' talk football all night there's no point in avin-a telly as background, is there?' She never gave up. I could see where I got it from.

My dad switched over and we went to the kitchen for a 'team talk'. My mam thought football was preventing me doing my school work and she was right. My dad had been a really skillful player, or so he constantly said, but never made it cos he'd 'gone on the pop'. (I used to wonder how coke and lemonade could've had such an effect!) All his ambitions went into me. It was odd cos he'd tried with my brother Darren, but Daz had rebelled. Now he was all 'booze 'n' birds' and my dad had furious arguments with him about wasting his life. He'd kicked him out loads of times. My mam taking him back out of pity for his state.

'Listen, Trace. Yew give im back all yew get, right? Carn yew play fera school?'

'Dad mun! Ee won' even say tha much. Ee'll jes look sorta smug as if t' say we'll ammer yew this season an yew carn even play ... an it's a bloody same with-a school team an all.'

'But ... 'ey ave girls' teams up 'ere now, don' 'ey?'

'Yeh, but it int-a same. I wanna prove t' tha Neil James that I'm as good as im!'

'Course yew are, Trace. Better in fact. Ee on'y got picked fera County coz tha Morgantown trainer drinks with the bloody selectors!'

I hated crying. It was too weak, but I thought I was going to 'do a Gazza'. He stood up and put an arm round my shoulder. He patted me awkwardly. He always found contact difficult.

'Trace! Yew'll show em, love. I know yew will.'

As tears got ready to flood, I channelled them. It was like in nightmares when I used to clap hands to escape. Now I made the water into welling lava. I was red hot and burning my way to the sitting-room, switching the telly back to *Sgorio* as mam protested (some couple had been undressing).

I was Vinnie the Ug stamping on heads up the stairs. I grabbed my Puma Kings and hurled them downstairs. That wasn't enough though. I took out those Southampton pennants and scissored them into tiny pieces over my bedroom carpet.

My parents knew better than to intervene. My mam waited for the eruption to end – or the next commercial break – and then came up to tell me off.

She was in a better mood than expected, but I was determined to do the opposite to what she said. As I lay on my bed panting as if I'd played flat out for ninety minutes, she sat near me. When she cwtched me, it seemed genuine.

'Trace love, yew jest afto stop dreamin. Do yewer

school work an play for Cwmtaff Ladies when yew get bigger. Yew never know, the way thin's are, 'ey could be professional soon.'

'Okay, mam.' I couldn't be bothered to argue any more.

'An try an clear up tha mess on the floor an all.'

She left. She'd done her bit. The moaning started again downstairs. I'd behave as if the rules didn't exist. Frankie Hughes had done it all his life, so why couldn't I? Frankie was my hero, even though he could be a right sod. He was a nutter. He didn't care what anyone said. He'd been kicked out about five times by the Committee and they had to have him back cos the parents created hell. He was the finest trainer in Cwmtaff.

In school, Neil James hardly spoke to me, thank God. He was occupied with a rock magazine, which had some stupid name like *Gunge*. Gary Crissle was really kind and told me I'd walk into Year 10 Girls no problem. I bothered with his younger brother Ryan, or 'Giggsy'. I found most girls' talk boring. I had no interest whatsoever in why Robbie left Take That or which Year 11 boy was the lushest. Me and Giggsy talked football every second we were together. We picked our fantasy Premier team and tried not to include too many Man. Utd players. Gary sometimes came over and rabbited about Carlo Corazzin.

'Oo's ee when ee's at ome?' I teased.

'On'y the tops. There's big teams arfta im an all.'

'Wha? Brighton?'

Gary told me training was tomorrow lunchtime and Mr Jewell was taking it. Jewell was a right MCP! I didn't stand a chance! He'd even stopped Gemma Evans playing rugby and she'd been Player of the Year for the town Under 13's.

When the session came, I was convinced someone would grass me up. Probably Neil James would do it casually, like ... 'Sir, is there a girls' team in Year 9?' to draw attention to me being there.

Luckily, there were so many in the Sports Hall Mr Jewell didn't notice. I was the only girl in Year 9 who didn't want her tits to grow big as a Page Three. My hair was centre-parted and similar to a few boys' styles. Also, I'd changed it since all that stuff on the telly. I reckon nobody grassed cos they wanted an excellent team.

Jewell chose teams by numbers not captains, so my name wasn't called out. When a player called for the ball it would be a problem. I was in the same team as Gary, who wasn't great, but had a go. As we sat on a bench waiting to play, I told him to brief the others. 'It's Terry. Orright?'

We faced real difficulties with Kevin Davies, our goalie. Basically, he was dull and, at the top of his voice, was shrieking at me, 'No problem at all, Tracey.... I mean Terry. Carn I call yew Ter, Trace?'

Even with the whistle echoing and the shouts of both teams from the first game, I was surprised Jewell didn't hear.

Fortunately, Kevin was so dull he hardly ever called in a game and spent his time trying to make dents in the Hall floor. We won our first two matches and I scored five. Jewell even came over and asked my name. 'Terry James!' I announced, grinning and glad Neil was out of range.

We met Neil's team in the final and he was ready to show who was Number One. He scored their first, when Kev flung the ball straight at him.

'Kevin Davies! You're like an ol woman!' yelled Jewell

and James was smirking. He approached me and whispered: 'We're gunna ammer yew ... Terry.'

But I set up Gary for an easy goal and there were only a few minutes left. If it went to penalties we didn't stand a chance as their keeper, Wayne Jenkins, was in the school team. Jewell wanted to go for his dinner, he kept glancing at his watch all the time.

I beat James to a fifty-fifty, dashed for goal and walloped it with my left. Just in! Our team mobbed me, a bit too closely for my liking, especially Gary.

'Crissle, if I didn't know better, I'd think you were one o' them!' said Jewell, subtle as ever.

When the whistle went, James was seething. He came up and shouted, so Jewell could hear clearly: 'Well done, Tracey! Pity girls can't play in-a school team, in it?'

Jewell eyed me up and down. The last of the players were leaving the Hall, but he made it public.

'Oh, s' you're tha Tracey Estebanez, eh? Well, I've heard of a boy named Sue.... You're a great player, girl, but yew shouldn be here. You should join Mr Bryn Jones' Year 10 Girls. You'll get in tha team easy.'

James was hanging about by the door, waiting for my reaction.

'Sir! I'm as good as any boy yer an I proved it today. Yew don' pick me fer-a team an tha's yewer problem!'

Just as he was saying 'Don' give me lip!' I hurried out the Hall, elbowing James – who actually gave me an admiring smile – on the way.

That evening I played on the Greens with Giggsy and Gary. As me and Giggsy took turns to shoot at Gary in goals, he said: 'Trace, there's no way Jewell'll let you in the team. Y'know what ee thinks about mixed sports.

That girl Gemma's a brill prop – built like a JCB – an ee won't pick er.'

Giggsy piped in: 'Yer, Trace, wish I'd seen your winnin goal. Bet it woz epic!'

I tried to chip Gary and failed.

'Anyroad, I don' give a monkeys. I'll play f' Penôl. Frankie'll let me.'

Gary threw the ball to his brother, who did a few kickups, showing off his ability.

'Well, best o' luck, Trace!' said Gary. 'C'mon you little nerd. Get on with it!'

He dived for Giggsy's swerving shot and landed in dog-shit, missing the ball. We laughed our heads off, as he wiped his hand in a clump of grass and then tried to wipe off a smear on his number 9 Butler shirt.

'Always knew yew woz shit!'

Gary ran after his brother trying to boot his arse. Giggsy was too fast and Gary gave up.

When it got too dark to play on, we exchanged so longs and Gary said how he'd like to get in the Penôl team as well.

'It'd be great if you could beat Morgantown. Tha James is such a posh get!'

'Night Terry!' Giggsy giggled cos Gary had told him everything.

As I cheerfully winged home, I practically knocked into this drunken bloke down an alley.

'Ey! Watch it sonny!'

I was pleased to be mistaken. It was safer that way.

Two days to Penôl training. I hadn't been this season, but knew from Wayne Jenkins that they were struggling to get a team. Frankie attracted players, but his assistant Geoff 'the Teeth' Reynolds put off as many. Geoff was in charge of fixtures and would've liked to pick the team, but Frankie would have none of it. He stood on the touchline every game, slagging off every player except his son, Phil, who was a solid tackler, but couldn't pass to our team. I'd played since I was seven and mostly we'd been pipped by Morgantown for the League, but had won the Cup last season.

Frankie was magic. I could rely on him. He'd stick a chipolata down my shorts if necessary. I focussed my mind on our future meeting with Morgantown, our rivals. James tried to be pleasant in school, but I brought him down with a two-footed tackle.

'Yew lost, Jamesy. An yew couldn take it!'

Whatever he said after was bull and he knew it.

Thursday came and I was early. I wished Gary was there for company, but I think he knew Frankie wouldn't put up with his lack of pace. Giggsy was too young.

When Geoff 'the Teeth' drove up with his boy, I feared the worst. He was on the Committee and loved rules. Phil was in full Newcastle kit. He supported who-ever was top and had a different kit for each session. I hadn't seen him over summer, as he went to Afon Comp down the valley.

'Hi, Tracey! Pity about Southampton, eh?'

'Balls, Phil!'

'What?'

'Balls an pennants an tha. Tha's all I got from em. Oh, an a kiss from Matt Le Tissier.'

'Wish I'd ad a chance like tha.'

'Wha? Yew fancy Matt an all, d' yew?'

He blushed and went over to the pitch, pretending to

test it by toeing boots into the turf.

His dad hung around, staring at me as if I'd grown a Jimmy Hill beard. Phil soon got fed up and got a ball from his car-boot. We passed and hardly talked, till others joined us, including Wayne Jenkins. We milled around and took shots at goal.

Frankie was always late. Once, against Pwll, Geoff 'the Teeth' had picked the team cos Frankie hadn't turned up. He put me as sub. We'd just kicked off when Frankie arrived, beerbelly spilling over tracksuit bottoms. He was unshaven and must've slept in the shed. He put me on straight away and Reynolds was ripping. I scored a cracker for Frankie that day. I nearly gave 'the Teeth' a two-finger salute!

Frankie's skip of a Fiat pulled into the car-park. Reynolds hi-jacked his attention from us and they were deep in conversation, Frankie using his hands like an Italian player complaining to the ref. I thought he'd won when Reynolds glared over and threw his head back in disgust.

Frankie didn't talk to me, didn't single me out. He swore at the lot of us and had us lapping the field, jumping up for headers, touching the ground and dodging. It was brill! I was part of the squad. Not a girl, not Tracey Estebanez hits the headlines, just 'Trace! Yew call tha runnin! I seen lame snails go faster 'an tha!' Frankie had played for some 4th Division team and Cwmtaff. Now, blowing a whistle made him sweat buckets. He was overweight and mouthy. Nobody crossed him. Geoff 'the Teeth' stood by the touchline checking forms, face long as winter rain.

At the end I was totally knackered. Fit for a week in bed. Geoff called us over to sign and took down everyone's details except mine. I pushed myself right in front of his miserable features and he ignored me. His teeth were like gravestones. Frankie came over with a bag of balls.

'Friendly against Cardiff team Saturday lads. Winston Park ... their League champions. Meet 'leven o'clock up yer, right?'

He saw my angry expression.

'Oh aye, an don' forget t' bring a saveloy, Trace. It's an ol trick.'

I immediately perked up.

'Chipolata, Frankie. I wuz thinkin o' that anyway.'

'Aye ... evr'yone signed up, Geoff?'

'Yeh, I think so.'

'Mr Reynolds! Wha about me?'

'Yew know the rules, Tracey. No girls allowed in the under 14's.'

'But...' I sought help from Frankie.

'Yew're playin Saturday, Trace. Beyond tha, I carn promise. ... I'm sorry.'

I swung my boot-bag in disgust and strode off. So much for Frankie Hughes! Thought he'd make a stand, but he was too scared they'd get expelled. For all I knew he'd played along with the Southampton scout, knowing full well I'd be rejected when they found out.

I'd changed in rat-ridden cupboards and shared kitchens with droppings of tea-bags which stuck to my socks. I'd changed in bogs with smells worse than stink-bombs. For his team, I'd put up with taunts of 'Yew a lezzy 'en?' when players I marked found out. Frankie cheered my every tackle, every move, to send my confidence flying. But now, let's face it, I was on my own.

I would win. I'd turn up every game. I'd bring two

onion bhajis to go with the sausage. I remembered something from History about the suffragettes. They didn't accept things. They were force-fed and went to prison. They'd have to carry me from the touchline and lock me in the Ladies. They'd have to screw off my studs cos I don't wear them, they're extensions of my body. I slept with my first boots on, my dad told me. My mam says I kicked like a mule in her womb. I've been kicking ever since and I'll go on.

In the Graveyard

For me, this was an opportunity to investigate. For my parents, a chance to 'Carry On Giving Off' (they had their own series of films). As I got out the car at Ffynnon Church car-park, last night seemed continents away, but dad wouldn't stop lecturing me and mam kept echoing like the sheep across valley.

'Catherine! I still can't understand yew! It's not as if we aven't given yew any freedom.'

'Stop slopin off an listen t' yewer father!'

I envied Steve, my brother, off to college and my sister Diane living with her husband in Cardiff. For all Steve's landlord being Manchester's version of Marko Morgan (who owned all Cwmtaff's shady B 'n' B's), at least he didn't have to put up with them!

My dad, bald and bespectacled, sweated in the May sun and wiped his brow with a tissue. My mam – trying to dress young in jeans – wearing a permanent frown.

I loved this place and had done since a child, when my tadcu brought me here and I'd be free to roam and explore. Now it seemed to collide: last night, today, my childhood.

At the large, fenced-off grave I almost expected to see two marks on the stone, two shadows caught there. How were they to know? I stared at the inscription again. They trapped me, one each side. Once Steve left I was the centre of attention for the first time. I felt flattered by it but also, as now, a squeezing of breath.

'Catherine....' My mam began talking this time. I disliked the longer, formal name as much as I despised the shortened 'Ca' some friends used in school. I heard snippets of what she was saying, but drifted back.

'Don' ruin yewer life....' Going out with Neil had been the start. 'I've always regretted not stayin on in school....'

He was bright and bold and had a vision to escape. I caught snatches of my dad. ... 'We on'y want what's best for yew....' For a man with qualifications, he had a fine line in clichés. Neil and I so different: he wanted away and I was attached to the history. 'Yew're really weird, Cath Jones!' he'd say. But Neil turned out to be all self; wanted his own way. Then it was Gavin, so different again. The school production. The party after. Amazed at a sixth former giving little old me so much time.

GODFORGIVEME

I read once more.

'I've done nothin wrong!'

'Yew lied to us!'

What had Robert Johnson Crayshaw got to hide? My tadcu from the Blaen was an excellent local historian and had told me about a casket in Cymer Castle (home of the Crayshaws) which would reveal everything. According to a will, it couldn't be opened till later this century. But, by that date, the secrets would have rotted! 'Maybe we'll never know,' my tadcu's hoarse voice scarred by years of the dust, scratched at the gravestone. Now he was ill and stuck in a Home, not remembering who we were when we visited.

I turned away and went towards the tombs and the small charnel-house (I think that's what tadcu had called it). I searched the path, the graves, the grass, looking for clues.

*

103

Gav picked me up at the top of our street. I'd arranged my alibi with Helen. If they phoned she knew what to say. She was no actress, but could manage to lie for once. It was risky, but hopefully my mam wouldn't phone and ask to talk. If she did, Helen would pretend to call me and say I was on the toilet.

I felt deceitful and delighted. It was like eloping, but Gavin was calm and let me speak, rushing and bubbling, a stream in flood.

'I carn believe this, Gav. Ow did yew get yewr dad's car? Where we off 'en? They bought my story perfect an I even got a sleepin-bag. Wonder what we cun do with it?'

We'd met like that: me jabbering and him making the occasional remark. Almost everyone fancied him, even Helen who hadn't thought about boys since Liam Connell's suicide. After the school production, *Our Day Out*, I'd got my hands on smuggled cider. I wasn't exactly a seasoned drinker and it went to my head, limbs and other parts. It didn't take long before I was all over Gavin, sitting astride him and loving those jealous eyes focussed on us.

'Cathy, yew woz bloody great as Carol, onest.'

I drank up his compliment like the last dregs from the flagon. I'd been so accustomed to Steve getting all the praise in our house. Gav's bass tones went through me like sadly joyful chords.

And here he was, driving me out of town.

'Don worry Ca, we'll jest go fer-a quiet drink in the Pont.'

He sounded so experienced, so mature. His eyes were reassuring. He wanted me to trust his motives, but truthfully I didn't care as long as he didn't go straight down some lane, or to any pubs in town where his mates or my dad's colleagues would go.

'Yew talkin t' me, Gavin Price, or t' this vehicle yer?'

'Oh sorry, Cathy, I forgot.'

He wasn't brash and big-headed like Neil could be. Playing Colin, the young teacher, he'd nearly been acting himself when the two schoolgirls flirted with him. For someone so good-looking, why was he so modest?

'So wha's yewr fault 'en Gav?'

'Ow d'yew mean?'

'Well, I've yet t' find wha's wrong with yew. There mus be summin!'

'Yew'd be amazed....'

'Yew're not gunna turn like one o' them psychos in films ,I ope. Go all loopy an and end up jumpin off of a buildin with-a cops arfta them.... There's always the viaduct.'

He turned into the pub's car-park and stopped the car. He deliberately bulged his eye-balls and strained to put on a maniacal voice.

'Ca! Tha's all yew are is jest a car to me!... I will take yew apart an put yew together again!'

He grabbed my thigh. I let out a sharp scream, at the same time snortling laughter.

As we crossed to the Pont, hand in hand, I asked.

'Think I'll get in orright, Gav?'

He withdrew his hand, stopped and surveyed me head to toe, taking me all in.

'Not enough make-up, Cathy. Yew shoulda slapped more on. I gotta friend oo's a plasterer ... ee could of obliged.'

'Be serious, Gavin. An supposin my dad's up yer ... ee could be avin a secret affair with is secretary.'

'In which case, no problem ... yew'll be able t' black-mail im!'

There were no hassles for us and nobody familiar was there either. Gav drank shandy very correctly and I had halves of cider to bring back our first meeting. We had a great laugh recalling the animals from the production that our brave producer Ms Dawkins had used in the zoo scene.

One night, the rabbit shat all over Wayne Griffiths and he'd shaken droppings over the stage. Better still, the hamster disappeared up Bethan Reilly's jumper and during the bus scene she'd done this weird hip-hop dance to try and extract him. In the end, he'd flown head first out of her sleeve and landed on the stage, only to bolt to the wings, causing mayhem amongst the stage-helpers. The RSPCA could've sued the school for thousands!

We cwtched up in the corner and I could've stayed there till closing time, but Gav was getting bored with drinking shandy. After a few games of 'tonsil tennis', he was rising to the occasion so to speak.

'Le's go, is it Cathy?'

'Gav! I still don' know wha yewr one big weakness is.'

'Promise I'll show yew later, right?'

'Promise? ... Well, where shell we go? My place t' meet the folks, or an istorical tour of Ffynnon Church?'

'Yeh, why not?'

'Yew wha? I woz on'y jokin Gav.'

'Le's go for it! Ffynnon Church. At least it's different. I cun tell my mates on Monday ... rave in a grave. 'Ow about it?'

'Okay ... are yew prepared?'

'No prob. Why d'yew think I wuz so long in-a bogs? I knew there wuz a machine up yer.'

'Oh, I see. Come yer reg'lar, d' yew?'

'Cathy! I int a babe!'

'No, but I am.'

The windy road to the church was like a tunnel, despite the clear starry night: the stone walls very high. Gav drove carefully. My chatter overflowed with added cider.

'Maybe we'll meet Crayshaw's ghost. Ee's buried up yer ... the last one oo ewsed t' live in Cwmtaff. My tadcu reckoned ee wuz a real wrong un – tha's ow ee put it. Ee done all kindsa things with is maids ee tol me.'

'Could be better 'an a blue movie!'

'Ah! I've found it!'

Gav pretended to look for something I'd lost.

'Wha?'

'Yewr vice, o' course. Naughty films, is it?'

'No way. Snow White turns me on.'

For the first time, we were both silent, as he steered into the deserted car-park. The tyres on gravel grated my nerves. The graveyard was eerie behind mossy walls. The moon made that peculiar wooden-roofed church glow.

'Bring yewr rucksack, Cathy!' Gavin commanded.

'What for? We campin?'

He faced me, his expression earnest, as he picked at the skin of his fingers.

'Cathy, yew wanoo, don yew?'

I teased him, 'Want to wha, Gavin Price? I thought this wuz 'n istorical tour?'

'Okay! If tha ... le's go then!' he was on the verge of starting the car.

'C'mon, Gav. I wuz avin yew on. Don' be s' serious all of a sudden.'

I grabbed my rucksack and we stepped quietly out the car.

'Now yew know my one big fault,' whispered Gavin.

'Sokay, I seen it all evenin!'

We caught hold of each other as we approached the gate. He was more relaxed now, while I was beginning to shake. It was chilly, but more than that I was afraid of disappointing him. He must have been with loads and I was so inexperienced.

He pulled and pushed at the latch. His clumsiness made me feel better.

'Ope yewr better with bra-straps!'

'I wouldn know 'bout such thin's!'

I took him over to Crayshaw's grave.

'God forgive me, Gav.'

'Why, what ave yew done?'

'Na! There! Look!'

'Oh aye. Not exactly a fancy gravestone, is it?'

I thought I could hear voices rising from the valley's bottom, but soon dismissed them as we kissed. I felt daft with my rucksack on. I kept thinking of an African woman with her baby for some reason. We held really tight and warm and soon his hands were slipping into my blouse.

'Ouch! Yew're bloody freezin!'

'Sorry!'

He drew back his head, studying my expression.

'Cathy?'

'Yeh?'

'What would yew say if I suggested kippin on tha grave in yewr sleepin-bag?'

'Yew dirty bugger! Tha's wha's bin on yewr mind.'

'Now yew know my foible.'

'I aven even touched it!'

'Na ... foible ... weakness ... my passion f' 60's films.'

His earth-coloured eyes glinted with cheekiness, a pebble shine in soil.

'Eh?'

'*Easy Rider* ... sex in-a graveyard.'

'Oh, yewr so romantic Gavin! Orright! Le's try an wake ol Crayshaw eh?'

I thought I heard distant talking again, but my heart was louder as I unpacked the sleeping-bag and we climbed on to the gravestone. Gav glanced down valley, where the path led, but the sound had abated.

With clothes still on, we huddled into the bag together. It reminded me of telly pictures of John Lennon and Yoko Ono, only a lot more respectable. It was too cold to strip off, thank goodness. It was a double bag, so there was enough space. We were side on and Gav kissed my neck and forehead.

He was slobbering a bit, but I didn't mind.

Just as we were sighing, excited, catching every breath, there was a chanting from quite close by, near the charnel-house. Gav didn't appear to notice, his hand wriggling into the back of my skirt.

'Gav! Wha's that?'

'Eh? ... It's on'y my and!'

I sat up.

'Wha's-a matter Cathy?'

Now he sat up too, listening to the same chants, sounding like a prayer. Walking up the path to the charnel-house, we saw shapes of people holding candles. They were darkly-dressed and hooded. The chant became more like a moan, till it was shattered by the scream of some animal, cat or bird. The people gathered round the charnel-house, their flames in a semi-circle.

Gavin grabbed my arm.

'Le's go Cathy! Quick!'

I tried to stuff my sleeping-bag into the rucksack and a few things fell out.

'Gav, give us an and will yew?'

We scrambled around on all fours, retrieving my toothbrush and toothpaste, which I'd packed just in case. We hopped over the grave-railings and clanked noisily through the gate. They were far enough downhill, but must have heard. Though they were silent now, I expected them to bound after us, as Gav fumbled with his carkeys, muttering 'Shit, shit, shit!'

In at last and in the headlights we saw people in black cloaks, one carrying a large silvery object. Faces white under the moon, contrasted with what they wore.

He accelerated away and we laughed with relief.

'I'd 've rather met bloody Crayshaw's ghost!'

'P'raps yew did! Oo the ell were they, Cathy?'

'Ell's right! Devil-worshippers? Were they real or wha?'

He went quiet; brooding on a missed opportunity no doubt.

I was equally upset. It would've been so dramatic making it on that grave. Something to tell my grandchildren about.

'Cun yew come t' my ouse, Cathy?'

My watch said five past twelve. I couldn't exactly wake up Helen and demand a bed.

'What about yewr parents Gav?'

'It's Saturday, Cathy. They'll be in bed. They go up-a club an they'll be deep in a pissed sleep. I'll smuggle yew in, okay?'

'Aye, why not?'

He smiled wide as a gorge.

'Them devil-worshippers looked really weird, din 'ey? Cloaks an all. They woz problee sacrificin summin. Don' yew think we should tell-a cops?'

'Na, they'd think we woz off ower eads, Cathy.' He put on a stage-policeman's voice, '"And what were you doing at Ffynnon Church at 12 midnight, sir?" "Oh, jest makin love on Crayshaw's grave, tha's all, officer." "I see, desecration of holy places. I'm afraid I'll have to arrest you both. Lucky if you get life for this."'

He was hilarious. I couldn't wait to get to his house. It was in Chapel Street and not far away.

Thankfully, there were no signs of life when we arrived. But as soon as we'd opened the door, there was 'Gav!' from the kitchen. I could've escaped, but a moment later, his mam emerged in dressing-gown. She gazed past him at me, standing like a delivery person in the doorway.

'Are yew Cathy Jones?'

She was cross and liquidy-eyed, sobered up against her will.

'Coz I've ad a phone call from yewer dad. Apparently, ee thought yew woz stayin with someone called 'elen. ... Ee went round this 'elen's with yewer nightie, which yew'd forgot.'

As she told the story she livened up. At the same time, I was full of dread.

'Well this 'elen give im ower number. Well, it didn take me long t' work out. ... Yew'd better phone ome now.... Gavin! Yew get straight t' bed, d' yew yer?'

I couldn't believe how sheepish he became. He gave me a quick wave and a 'S'long' and obediently went upstairs.

'Yeh, thanks fer the evening, Gav!' I said to his heels.

'An ow old are yew, Cathy?'

She looked as if she knew already.

'Fourteen, Mrs Price.'

She shook her head and showed me to the phone.

'I would never let my girls carry on like tha!'

She left me and returned to the kitchen.

Our phone only rang a second. My parents must've been standing ready. My dad was livid. I couldn't get a word in.

'Yew come ome now, my lovely girl. Make no mistake about it, yew'll be grounded for a considerable time for this. I'm absolutely disgusted! Yewr mother's been cryin all night. Yew'll make er ill, that's what yew'll do. I ope yew're satisfied! Where've yew been all this time? Out drinkin?'

He actually paused for a reply.

'Yeh ... I mean ... on'y a couple. We went fera drive. Me an Gavin, ee's. . . .'

'A drive? Till arfta midnight? Yew're lyin t' me, Catherine. An yew won be goin out again till we get the full story!'

I examined the area around the charnel-house carefully. No stubs of candles, no drips of wax and no dead bodies of virgins or black cats!

My parents joined me, not leaving me alone for long. My mam held up my hairbrush to my nose.

'Oh!' I tried not to seem startled. 'Ta mam. Where d'yew find it 'en?'

'Up by-a side o' tha grave yew wuz lookin at before.'

'Musta fallen from my pocket.' I placed it in my jeans pocket, letting it hang out a bit, even though it could've fitted well in. I pushed open the charnel-house door and entered. The tombs were mostly soiled and worn, but on one, the largest, I saw clean scrapings under the weighty top stone.

Dad followed me in and he must've seen them too.

'Looks as if Dracula woz out for a bit last night!' he joked, the first time he'd been pleasant all day.

'Yeh ... creepy! ... d'yew believe in black magic dad?'

'On'y the chocolates, Cathy. Now, we'd better be off. Yewr mam can't stand places like this, they give er the shivers.'

He cleaned his specs, as if those marks were on them and could be wiped off.

We trundled back to the car-park and he attempted a gentler line of questioning. I wasn't forthcoming. I was thinking too much about Gavin and whether we'd get together again. My parents (and probably his) would be dead against us. I loathed being fourteen: seen as their girl still, needing protection. They could ground me for two years, but they wouldn't keep me in. Next time, we'd choose a safer place: some old slag-heap or an abandoned farm.

End of the 32B Gang

I haven't waited so long since my first dental appointment. The tea tastes like bog water! A WPC stands by the door, as though I'm going to make a run for it. Who shot the sheriff? Not me, I'm innocent. My dad's a solicitor, I know about it: Birmingham 6, Guildford 4 and now the Cwmtaff 1. It seems piddling compared to them.

It's bizarre! There's a whole choir in the next room. They've been singing all the time. Most of their songs sound foreign, African I think, though some are in Welsh. Why arrest a choir in Cwmtaff of all places? Mind, I'd like to arrest some of those Male Voice jobs for their boring ancient hymns.

My dad's on his way. I'll be rescued like Olive Oil in Popeye. And mam's on her way too. If they meet it'll be hell. They'll be so busy targetting blame, they'll forget I'm here, innocent.

The choir launches into a stirring song which reminds me of that film, *Cry Freedom*. The WPC tries to put me at ease by saying at least there's free entertainment. Then I remember passing those singers once down town by Tesco's, protesting about apartheid.

'Scuse me!'

'Yes?'

'Why were they arrested?'

'I'm not shewer. Obstruction I think.'

I envy their togetherness, their harmony. A deep bass reverberates and I shut my eyes, imagining I'm in South

Africa and taken in for marching with the blacks, for stoning the police.

That song from Limbowander comes back to me and I think of myself as their new, young songwriter, discovered while they were gigging around Wales, once rock's forgotten country. I make up words:

Stuck in a police cell
Innocent and playing hell -
Songs of freedom
Another country far away -
Their struggle and mine
We've been betrayed

The 32B gang. That was us. Not named after a bus, but a bust! We all wore the same size bra at the same time. We were close as sisters ought to be. In school we cheated in tests telepathically. We copied homeworks and made subtle changes to fool teachers. We loathed Take That and when Blur and Oasis came, wrote them on our foreheads. The new Beatles. After a while, you had to choose between them. At that point, I began to change.

I was losing a constant battle with my body. No sooner had I punctured spots than others would appear, like molehills on a lawn. My periods would creep up on me and I'd bleed unprepared at school, having to stuff half-used tissues down my knickers to stem the flow. My legs began to grow too long for my body, so I resembled Looby Lou in that stupid kids' programme my dad watched for old time's sake. I tried to shave them with my dad's razor and cut myself. He thought I was into self-mutilation and hid it after.

My mam lives alone in a flat. She couldn't cope with

me and my younger brother Josh. She can't really manage herself to be honest, but I keep seeing myself in her, unable to look beyond the mirror. I'm petrified in case I turn out such a wreck.

I suppose I'd like to think it began with a video about meat production in Science. In fact, it was more to do with my crush on Dave Robinson, the young teacher. He was a Geordie who spoke like *Byker Grove*. The boys called him 'Gazza', but we called him P.J. after the singer. We being the 32B gang: Don, Mel, Rhi and me, Bec – as in Rebecca.

We thought he was lush and chattered too much to get attention. We'd also behave badly to get into detention, especially Melanie, who knew how to wind him up. In the middle of a lesson on human anatomy, she'd ask the most dopey questions. Things like, 'Sir, where do the wax in yewer yers come from?' and 'Ow come boys fluff more 'an girls?' Her interest in bodily functions infuriated him. Eventually, he told her to shut up and she'd sulk and ignore him completely. Sometimes, if she was lucky, he'd put her in detention. At other times – especially when she was going to be the only one there – he'd pretend to forget she'd ever done wrong. I felt sorry for him, because he went so red when he was angry I thought he'd burst and we'd have to collect his bits for dissection. Anyway, I'd have picked up his gorgeous parts and put them together!

This particular lesson we watched a video which showed chickens in battery farms, pigs rammed into cage-like things and abattoirs and factories where animals were slaughtered. It was appallingly cruel. Mel acted sick and asked to go to the bogs immediately or 'I'll spew over yewer nice new jumper sir!'

It had a powerful effect on me. We had a discussion

and it was obvious that Mr Robinson favoured eating animals as long as they roamed freely. I saw it differently and spoke out – I don't often, but when I do I make it count.

'Sir! Wha difference does it make? It's like angin or the electric chair. We jest shouldn kill any f' meat. Simple as that!'

'You a vegetarian then, Rebecca?'

'No, but ... I'd like t' be.'

The rest of the 32B gang (most now bigger) tittered. I glared at Donna and Rhian, who seemed glad to see Dave Robinson show me up. At that moment I went off him. He posed as a champion of animals and the environment, but he didn't care enough. 'I'll show em.' But I wasn't ready to give up those tasty burgers or tandoori chicken yet.

I was waiting for a sign. You may think I'm daft, but I do believe in such things. We did this Shakespeare speech once and Mr Thomson said one thing I remember: it was about ravens being prophecies of doom.

For me it was a sheep, not a raven. Me, dad and Josh were up the Beacons. We'd found a deserted farmhouse and Josh was ecstatic about an old car, pulling at its rusty doors. I wandered into the house itself and saw it hanging over a window-space. It looked recently killed. There was a smear of blood from its mouth which stained the wall. It reminded me of a butcher's shop, carcasses hooked and bled of life. Its wool was smudged red and eyes were coins of white.

I left, briskly walking down the forest path. It was a while before dad realised I'd gone, he was so busy entertaining Josh.

'Becky, what's up? Wait for us!'

When they caught up, Josh was complaining and accusing me of spoiling his fun.

'Jest coz I woz avin a good time, dad. She's a pain!'

'Yew're the pain. Yew don understand nothin!'

'Becky, please. What about an explanation?'

Stopped, told him head on, 'Dad! I never wanna eat meat again!'

That same week the raven worked once more. Late at night I was messing with my ghetto-blaster. I twirled the dial, trying to find some interesting music. I got a station which sounded Dutch and heard the name Limbowander.

The music was something else! It matched the name: trumpets, female vocalists, a man rapping and samples all in one, a collage of sounds. Limbowander weren't the new Big Flood, they were themselves. At first, I couldn't make out a single word. Josh disturbed me by yelling from his room.

'Dad! Tell Becky! Tell er, dad! I carn get t' sleep. She's playin it too loud!'

Dad was on the phone downstairs and ignored Josh's whining.

Josh slammed his door shut, loud as a gun-shot. I began to pick up pieces of the song. They were singing it for me.

Kept in cells, beaks clipped
Who is to blame, who is wrong?
On the plates there are no faces
No eyes are left, no song.

The chorus, chanted again and again. The radio croaked, but this was a dove not a raven. The girl singer cooed, the rapper spat. My dad shouted for me to turn it down. They announced it as 'Abattoir Assassins'. I switched it off, amazed and forever changed.

The girls didn't take long to notice. We met down town for a coffee in Jake's. Mel encouraged us to vote for either Blur or Oasis. I acted not to care, dreaming through the window, eying the talent they'd think.

'C'mon Bec. Oo d' yew support?'

'Mel, yew know I ate football.'

'I swear yew int from 'is bloody planet, Rebecca Phillips!' said Donna, 'we're talkin groups yer!'

'Yeh, c'mon Bec, it's two t' one,' urged Rhian.

I weighed things up, as dad might do in court, anticipating reactions.

'Okay, I'll tell yew then. I like Limbowander, tha's oo!'

'Oo?' Don laughed viciously.

Mel thought I was joking and carried on, 'It's gotta be Blur or Oasis, Bec. We're gonna get the latest by the winner, yew gotta...'

'I abstain!'

'Oh, ark at miss fancy knickers yer. Jest coz yewr ol man's a bleedin lawyer!'

'Shut it, Don!' Mel tried to keep us united, also she favoured Blur, 'two t' one, Blur win. Nex Saturday we get their CD. Agreed?'

She included me in her gaze. I nodded to please her. I didn't want to lose them that easily.

At home I kept to my word, though Josh demanded bacon butties every morning to torture me and tandoori chicken for evening meals to make my cheese pastie look a solitary misery. To be fair, dad said he'd buy a Veggie Cookbook. I don't know why though, as we lived off take-aways and stuff my gran made.

I visited my mam midweek. She was in a state, so I didn't tell her anything. She moaned about my dad and how he'd flung her out. She was desperately lonely, but I couldn't blame him in a way. She used to trash the house regularly, her diet of Valium not strong enough.

Limbowander. Bet that name came to them in a dream. It sounded like their softer curves, not the knuckly side. I determined to try Cwmtaff's one decent music shop, imaginatively called 'Cwm Off It'.

Next Saturday I'd go for it, when the gang planned to buy Blur's *The Great Escape* – named after a pub in town, I told them. Only flutey-voiced Rhi believed me.

'Onest, Bec?'

We were down the Vans lunchtime, boosting spottiness with greasy chips.

'Yeh, coz they stopped an ad a drink there on-a way up north t' do a gig.'

In fact, if Blur had really passed through Cwmtaff on their world tour they'd have called the album 'THE EAT EAPE', on account of letters nicked from the sign.

'Give over, Bec!' Mel interrupted, fingering a lump of mad cow pie, which made me pleased with my decision. 'Anyway, oo are 'is Limbowhatyewmecall ... Limbo Dancers, is it?'

'Limbowander.... I yeard em on-a radio ... they woz mulin ... epic!'

'Bet theyer posh gets,' Don cut in, 'by the way, Bec, ow's yewer maid?'

'Yew mean my gran?'

'Na, I mean the woman oo does f' yewer dad.'

'Oh er? She's jest the cleaner.'

'Jest a f—in cleaner, is it? Well, my mam appens t' know er really well.'

'I mean, I like er.... Look, Donna, I carn elp what my dad does, right? Shell I tell im t' go on-a dole t' please yew, or wha?'

She turned away, more interested in a group of Year 10 boys. We agreed to meet down the bus-station that Saturday and go for a meal.

When we were eventually gathered at the bus-station, we had a mega-long discussion on where to eat. Mel favoured a pizza on a bench (it was a dry day), while Don and Rhi were determined to go to Burger Hall. Don had planned it to bug me, I'm sure.

'I int goin there. They chop down all-a rainforests fera start.'

'What for? T' make theyer cups an tha?' asked Rhi.

'Don' be soft! T' make theyer bloody veggie burgers from wood, o' course!'

Mel was getting fed up with the bickering.

'Look, Bec. They do veggie burgers there. S' le's jest go there, right?'

'S' what appened t' the pizzas?'

Mel wiggled her body like an old-time stripper.

'32B gang stick together, eh?'

What a joke! She was the biggest, well over 36!

'Okay, I'll do a deal.'

'Oh my God, listen t' daddy's girl!'

'Go on 'en, Bec!'

But Donna was already heading for Burger Hall. We tagged along behind.

'Right! We go t' Cwm Off It straight arfter. I cun look f' Limbowander an play it in-a shop. Okay?'

Donna swivelled round.

'Well, we're gettin Blur in Woolies, not there mind.'

'Why?'

'It's easier.'

'It's cheaper,' insisted Rhian.

The veggie burger was edible and I swallowed the temptation to have a go at them. It was frustrating, because Rhian's quarter-pounder with cheese looked scrumptious. With Josh it had been easier, I'd swat him with comments about BSE.

At Cwm Off It, the glum-faced owner sat behind his counter, fingering a magazine. He was darkly handsome and unshaven, but treated customers as if they were a liability.

I attacked the L's with gusto. The Limo Louts ... Lickspittle ... Lynyrd Skynyrd ... Def Leppard? Obviously the Def didn't count. The others ignored my quest, seeking posters of Liam Gallagher and Damon Albarn.

The owner actually resembled a raven, perched on a stool, pecking at articles. It was a bad sign. Mel came over at last.

'Any luck, Bec?'

'Na! I've even tried the J's an K's.... Nothin!'

'Shell I ask? Wha's-a name o' theyr album?'

By now, Donna and Rhian had joined us. Donna smugly smiling.

'They problee split arfta one single. Couldn stand-a sound o' therselves!'

I huffed over to Mr Moanyfeatures, who didn't look up.

'Got any tapes or CD's by Limbowander please?'

'Or vinyl,' said Don, getting a response with her sarkiness.

'Oo?'

'Limbowander.'

'Never yeard of em!'

Don and Rhi smirked. Mel defended me again.

'Well, carn yew look em up in a catalogue or summin?'

He strained himself to stand up.

'So wha's theyr latest?'

'Er....'

'They've got a song called "Abattoir Assassins" ... could be theyr single.'

'Wha's-a label?'

'Look! D'yew wanna know ow old they are as well?'

'Orright, orright.... I'll ave a look.'

When he disappeared into the back, I noticed Rhi and Don nervously handling CD singles they'd taken from a box on the counter. Don took one and held it, as if checking its weight. Mr Sulkysocks returned with a thick catalogue and she popped it back in the box. He licked his fingers like a bank-clerk.

'Now ... s' le's see.... "Abattoir Assassins". Funny title tha. Sounds dead cheerful!'

He'd soon skimmed through and slammed the catalogue shut.

'No sign of em.'

That was it. Dismissed. I was depressed. You couldn't buy a thing in Cwmtaff, it was a glorified slag-heap! Don humoured me.

'Ne' mind Bec. Buy Blur instead. Arfta all, yew got enough money.'

In Woolies, the gang took ages. I thought they were only going for Blur, yet they seemed to be reading the tracks on every Pulp, Oasis and Echobelly. I bought a box of After Eights as my dad had instructed. Josh would scoff the lot as always.

I went to find them and Don was suspiciously pleasant. She grabbed my bag and peered inside it.

'What yew got there, Bec? Ooo.... After Eights ... lovely!'

'Yer! Ave a look at this poster!' piped Rhi, showing me one of Jarvis Cocker performing strange acts with a banana.

Donna handed me back the carrier.

'S' when yew gettin Blur?'

'We'll leave it. Too expensive yer.'

'Yew wha?' said Mel.

'Yeh, le's try Smith's.' Don gripped Rhian's arm and they marched off through the automatic doors. As I followed, there was a furious bleeping. It sometimes happened in Cardiff shops and I didn't think anything. Don and Rhi quickened, giggling and whispering. A hand clamped me tight, pulled me round. Who the.... A security man. The bleeping was me! I dropped the carrier as if it was on fire.

'Yew'd better come with me!' He picked it up.

Mel was beside me, the other two didn't look back. I panicked, an insect quivering in a web.

'I never ... it's a mistake ... it's gotta be ... Mel?'

'Don' worry, Bec. It's problee them chocolates.'

Under arrest. A citizen's arrest (my dad had told me). Eyes of shoppers on me. Me! A criminal.

In an office the security man stood over. Mel kneeled and tried to console me, I knew it was an error. I wouldn't cry.

Soon a woman in a smart blue suit arrived, with the tag Marlene/Manager on her. She had no sympathy. She'd seen my kind before. I was guilty before she took the carrier and spilled its contents out: After Eights and...

124

a CD! "The Great Escape".

'Did you purchase both of these?'

She had me! Someone had put it there. I'd been framed.

'The CD ... it's not mine ... I don' even like em ... Blur I mean.'

'Look! I'm not here to discuss your musical tastes.'

'Give er a bloody chance!' Mel sprang to my defence. The security man even made a move towards her.

'Who are you?' snapped the manager.

'Er friend. Why?'

'And did you help her steal this?'

'No. ... I mean. ... I'm shewer she never....'

'Well, you'd better leave!.... Dave, escort her out please.'

Mel was ushered out, protesting. Security returned and stood over me again, as if I was going to lash out. The manager asked to see my receipt.

How the hell? Donna! She took my carrier. She was a slut!

She set me up!

'I didn nick it! I know oo did!' I blabbed, as she phoned the police.

The singing's more distant now. Most likely they're in a cell or cells. Pity Limbowander aren't here. They could use that choir on their next album (if they had one). I'd have to form my own band, call it Framed. My very first song would be 'Donna Slag', nastier than those Blur characters

Donna Slag built like a crag
Mugs her gran for a packet of fags

A knock and my dad appears. I hug him and cry for the first time since my ordeal. He keeps repeating 'There, there, Becky...' and patting me, like I'm a baby.

He persuades the WPC to leave us alone and we sit face to face. My solicitor now, not my dad. Grey hair, moustache, dark suit and formal tie make him official. He'll sort me out.

'Listen, Becky, it doesn't look great....'

'Dad, I never done nothin! Onest! This girl ... she planted it in my bag.'

'Who?'

'Donna Morris.'

'But isn't she supposed to be your friend?'

'Woz ... but wouldn er fingerprints be on it? Dad, why don' they get er?'

'They won't bother, love. As far as they're concerned you were caught red-handed. And anyway, they don't exactly like me.'

'Ow d' yew mean?' I was desolate.

'Remember that Russell Lewis case a while back?'

'I'm not shewer ... I think I can.... '

'He was up for assaulting a police officer. I got him off.'

'An did ee?'

'Maybe. That's not the point!'

'It is f' me.'

My head droops. I pick at the skin around my nails, tearing it for pain, hoping for blood. The Great Escape? Donna and Rhian. The ones who got away. I'd have a record. A stain I couldn't rub out. My fingers hurt. My dad says something about "a suspended sentence or a small fine".

I search the postered walls for a hopeful sign.

The Author

Mike Jenkins is an English teacher at a comprehensive school in Merthyr Tydfil. The author of six volumes of poetry, his work has been broadcast on radio and television. This collection of stories was written with the aid of an Arts Council of Wales bursary.